The Innocent Flower

Charlotte Armstrong

A BERKLEY MEDALLION BOOK
PUBLISHED BY
BERKLEY PUBLISHING CORPORATION

Copyright 1945 by Charlotte Armstrong Lewi

All rights reserved

Published by arrangement with Coward-McCann, Inc.

SBN 425-01860-1

BERKLEY MEDALLION BOOKS are published by
Berkley Publishing Corporation
200 Madison Avenue
New York, N.Y. 10016

BERKLEY MEDALLION BOOKS ® TM 757,375

Printed in the United States of America

BERKLEY MEDALLION EDITION, AUGUST, 1970
2nd Printing, November, 1970
3rd Printing, September, 1971
4th Printing, July, 1972
5th Printing, October, 1972

The fictitious characters of three of the children in this story are roughly drawn from three real children of my own. All the other characters are synthetic and do not represent, nor are they intended to represent, in any way any real persons.

Charlotte Armstrong

CHAPTER 1

Late one Sunday afternoon Mac Duff was poking the nose of his coupe along a side street in New Rochelle, groping for the Shore Road, when the hand of God came down and stopped him at Mary Moriarity's door.

What happened was that the summer rain, changing without any warning into a deluge, put an opaque wall of water all around the car. There was nothing to do but stop and pray that no other blinded car would blunder into him. Duff kept the motor running, but he turned off the windshield wiper since its gasps were desperate, disturbing, and futile. He listened to the weight of the rain. He thought the fact that he could feel it fall was all that made the difference between this and being at the bottom of a lake. He rather enjoyed the freakishness of the storm, the queer drowned light, the submerged sensation; but something about it scratched at his nerves just the same.

In three or four minutes the deluge was over, as suddenly as if the rent in heaven's belly had been zipped together. The pattering rain that kept on falling was like sunshine. As Duff's horizons cleared, he saw that he was parked a few feet ahead of a driveway, that in the driveway, in a car not more than thirty feet from where he himself sat, there had been sitting another man, whose startled and not-quite-unknown face looked back over his shoulder. Duff thought: The opposite of the aquarium; one caught land creature looks out of his dry tank and sees another.

The man climbed out, came quickly around a hedge, and opened Duff's door.

"I wonder . . ." he began. His eyeglasses had caught one drop which trickled eccentrically past his earnest eye. Duff, who was a noticing man, noticed that the head and shoulders thrust in so close were fairly dry. "I know who you are!" the man said, as if someone had accused him of not knowing. "You're MacDougal Duff. I don't know if you remember—"

"And you are the doctor with the Scandinavian name who testified in the Baxter case," said Duff pleasantly. "That's as close as I can come, sir."

"Christenson," said the doctor. "What I was going to say . . ." He flicked a glance down the street behind them. "I've got a little girl in here . . . want to get her to the hospital . . ." He spoke in spurts. Obviously, he felt hurried. "Going to take her myself, but water's got into my engine. Can't wait for the ambulance now. Want to get her out of the house before the Police Department shows up. . . ."

"Yes?" said Duff, lying low, not betraying his curiosity.

"A woman just died," the doctor said, with another frantic glance behind. "Taffy's got a temperature of a

8

hundred and four. Got to get her out of here. Have you got time to be a Good Samaritan? Have you got the gas?"

"Yes, of course. I'll take her."

"Good. Good. I'll tell her mother." The doctor went up the walk through the rain in a lumbering run with his head lowered.

In the street the water roared and whirled and gurgled, rushing back to the sea or the sewer. Duff raced his engine with a thoughtful toe. A woman has died and the police are coming. The old formula came irresistibly into his mind. That good old parade of interrogatives— What? How? When? Why? Who?

They carried the bundle between them and came at a half-trot. Duff had the door open. The woman got in. "All right, Norry, I've got her." The woman's hair was black, and her eyes were very blue.

"Mary, this is Mr. Duff. Mrs. Moriarity." The blue eyes scarcely saw him, and Duff said nothing but waded quickly around the car to the driver's seat.

"Don't worry," the doctor was saying, leaning in at the door. "I've called the hospital. They know what to do with you. I'll stay here, Mary. At least for a while. Send Eve back if you see her?" This was a question.

"I don't know," said Mary. "Are you all right, lamb?"

It seemed to Duff, as he got in, that the inside of his car was filled up with tenderness. The woman who sat beside him was weaving it like a warm cocoon around the child she held on her lap. About 95 per cent of her attention, and all of her nervous force, which Duff felt to be great, was turned to a loving, anxious prayer for the little girl in her arms. Duff felt the intensity of that

9

devotion. He considered himself its servant and waited quietly to be directed.

"If Constance comes, maybe she . . . ?" the doctor said and stopped, leaving it another question.

"I don't know," the woman said again.

She had pulled back a fold of cloth, and now Duff saw the little girl's face. The exquisite texture of her baby skin was flushed a clear rose, making her look vivid and beautiful. She had a straight little nose, powdered gold with freckles. Under her narrow golden brows, blue eyes, sleepy with fever, looked at Duff and accepted him. He could see the pulse in her temple beating hard where her fair hair swept back.

He said impulsively, "How are you, Taffy?"

Taffy put out her tongue and moistened her pretty mouth. "I'm just fine," she said.

The bachelor heart in Duff's scholarly breast turned over, nor was it ever the same again.

"God bless her," said Mary, "of course she's fine. Down to the corner, turn right. Then I'll tell you. It's not far."

The doctor slammed the door, lifted his hand like a salute, and let them go. They splashed through subsiding torrents. The rain was slackening. Trees looked washed.

"Is she very sick?" Duff asked quietly.

He felt Mary sigh and relax. "As a matter of fact, she's *not* . . . so very." Her voice was almost cheerful. "A high temperature doesn't mean much when they're little."

"How little is Taffy?"

"Taffy's seven."

"But you worry," Duff said.

10

"Yes, I worry. I don't know what I ought to do. I always stay with them when they're sick. I always do." There was a crooning anxiety in her voice. Duff was thinking that there must be healing power in such a loving presence, and so was she, because she went on, "I suppose it's silly. I suppose it's germs. I suppose all it takes is science."

"Who knows," said Duff, "whether that's all it takes? Lightning was all around us before we discovered electricity."

"Um, so it was," she murmured. "Turn left here. But the trouble is"—she blurted out her trouble—"I have five more children, and they home alone with a corpse! That isn't right."

Duff turned left very carefully and steadily. He cleared his throat, swallowing the faint sensation of shock. "No," he said, "that isn't right."

Mary made a little sound, part giggle and part gasp. "A friend, a guest in the house, died quite suddenly," she told him. "Just now." She rested her cheek on Taffy's head and seemed to brood. "My children have never seen death. I don't like to leave them with it. I don't like it myself. I . . . *hate* it! I ought to go back."

They crossed a business street and another and a railroad bridge. "Go around to the right," said Mary. "There it is. Do you see it?"

"Yes," said Duff. "I see it now. But they'll take her away, you know."

"I know," said Mary, "but in the nighttime . . . Oh, Lord, I love my children!"

Duff had a capacity for selflessly entering into whatever at the moment concerned a companion. He had a way of approaching a stranger on a level below

11

or deeper than ordinary. People often confided in him quite abruptly, as if they felt him to be really interested, or rather interested in what was real, as indeed he was.

But Mary Moriarity, herself, had put no separating nonsense between them. She hadn't said, "It's good of you to take the trouble . . ." He hadn't had to say, "Oh, no trouble at all." She hadn't said, "I don't know how to thank you . . ." He hadn't said, "Why, I'm glad to do it. Please don't mention it."

They had begun by not mentioning it and plunged directly into communication.

That was why, perhaps, Mary murmured as if she had forgotten he would hear, "I didn't want her to die. I didn't mean . . . to kill her."

"Of course not," Duff said promptly. "But was she killed?"

Mary was looking at Taffy, whose eyes were closed. "Well . . . poison . . ." she said.

Duff found his own way around a maze of corners and pulled up a little way from the entrance to the hospital building. Mary stirred. He held her by not moving. "I've had some experience with sudden death," he said casually, "quite a lot, in fact. I've dealt before with policemen and newspaper people and all of that. Would you mind if I went back to your house to help out the children? I am free. I could stay the night and keep bogey men away."

Mary Moriarity looked at him. His gray eyes were calm and friendly. "Please don't leave Taffy," he said. Then, deliberately, "I don't hate death any more than most."

Mary's eyes looked startled for an instant, and then they shone with sudden tears. She seemed shaken with relief. She gave a quick little nod of her head that held all the gratitude Duff ever wanted.

He smiled at her and got out and went around. She let him take Taffy, and they went into the hospital.

Duff carried his heavy, hot little burden down the corridor to her bed. They'd put her in a semi-private room, but the second bed was empty. Duff felt pleased. A nurse hovered. Her starch rustled at his back. The machinery of healing was impatient to take over. But Duff drew away very gently. Taffy was so quiet. Her blue eyes had no reproach for anything. She was sick as a little animal is sick, quietly, patiently, as if she knew it would pass . . . or it wouldn't. He kissed her limp little fingers and said, "Good night, Taffy."

"Good night," said Taffy serenely. She accepted without surprise this mystery of a tall kind man who had come from nowhere and carried her, and put her down so gently, and kissed her hands.

Mary was standing in the door of the room, talking to a woman in a blue and white nurse's aid uniform. ". . . vomited this afternoon," she was saying, "and now this fever. But the doctor didn't find anything. It's only because the house is upset. Eve,"—she put her hand on the woman's arm—"Brownie was taken quite suddenly. She's dead."

The nurse's aid was a thin, red-haired young woman who looked tense. She put up her hand as if to ward things off and gasped.

"Mary, what do you mean!"

"I know it's a shock," Mary said in hospital-hushed tones. "But it was a shock to everyone. We don't know, Eve. She was all right one minute, and the next . . ."

"My God," said Eve. "Oh, my God!"

13

Mary spoke sharply. "Will they let me stay here with Taffy? I want to stay here. They'll let me, won't they?"

"What? Oh, yes, I think so. Mary, how awful! Was it her heart?"

A dither, Duff thought, drawing closer. The dithering type, perhaps. He could see the cords in Eve's scrawny neck standing out.

"We don't exactly know," said Mary desperately and greeted Duff with her eyes.

The woman called Eve turned her head. Her skin was pale, with many tiny lines in it. Her teeth were outlined by the thin, fallen flesh around her mouth. Her eyes lay deep in her skull. The illusion of youth that came from her red hair and thin body was dispelled. She looked, close up, very like a death's-head.

"Eve, this is Mr. Duff. Mrs. Meredith, my neighbor."

"How do you do," said Eve in a high-pitched voice very artificially polite.

Duff bowed to her and said quietly to Mary, "How will I tell the children that I may stay? Can you give me any credentials?"

"Oh." Mary pushed a lock of black hair off her forehead. "Tell them," she said with a hint of mirth, "that your mother was one of the Mulligans."

"I'll tell them," said Duff solemnly. "I'm going back now."

Mary's mouth opened to say thank you, but she didn't say it. She looked pleased and excited, like one who had found arms to take against a sea of troubles. Duff went off down the corridor with a certain

jauntiness. He heard Eve Meredith's shr̶̶̶
behind him.

"Mary, who is *that!*"

Ah, who indeed? he asked himself.

He was in the elevator, going down, when the reaction came. What kind of sentimental old coot was he turning out to be? How in the name of any kind of common sense could he have been induced to promise to spend a night in a strange house with five strange children? Not to mention a corpse, who was strange, too. For what reason?

Because it had seemed to him that an appealing child needed her mother? Because Taffy was so obviously a darling, and her mother loved her so much? Yes. Yes. Even so. Or because Mrs. Moriarity hated and feared the presence of death in her house? Yet she would have gone back and covered over her fear to keep the kids from catching it. Oh, yes, all that. Even so, why should he, Duff, take it upon himself to spare her that ordeal and solve her problem? Mrs. Moriarity, surely, was not so devoid of friends or even, for all he knew, relatives, that she had to depend on someone plucked from the highway. Literally so.

As for that queer sense of unpremeditated friendship, that direct entering into the responsibilities of a friendly state, that discard of preliminaries, much as if they'd met on a battlefield . . . Pretty romantic, thought Duff. Some mystic nonsense or other. Mutual, though. There was the catch.

Of course, he conceded, coming earthward, the corpse was an attraction. A musician who stumbled over a grand piano in the backwoods, for instance, to run his fingers over the keys. private murder, you might say, had of Duff's time and thought than what use ent could make of his peculiar talents. He consulting, advising, snooping, and listening, for ferent kind of villainy.

Well, he was in for it. He felt he could permit himself to look forward to the corpse.

The lobby of the hospital was nearly deserted, but as Duff reached the doors to the street he caught up with a man and woman who paused, as he did, to look at the weather. It was raining again, and quite seriously.

The woman was young and upset. She had a bandage near her eye. The man was somewhat older. He held himself very erect with his head thrown back, and he was talking rapidly to her.

". . . get you home and have a stiff drink, I don't care what they say. Look, we don't have to wait for a cab. Wouldn't you rather walk? Get wet. It won't hurt us. Some fancy weather." He was batting his eyelashes at Duff in a friendly way.

"Very," said Duff agreeably.

"Lean on me, Bea. Say, didn't you come in with Mrs. Moriarity? Was it one of the kids?"

"Yes, it was Taffy," Duff said.

"Aw, too bad. My name's Walker. Used to know the family. I wondered . . . what's the trouble?"

"Why, I don't believe she's very sick," said Duff. "I think the doctor felt she'd be better off here."

"I see. That's good. We had a little smashup. Were you out in that cloudburst? Hit a fence, bunged up the car, but thank God I wasn't going very fast." The man seemed to be rattling along out of sheer nervous reaction. "Got to take the train back to the you haven't got a car, have you?"

"I have," Duff said.

The man looked at his watch. "Never mind. We have plenty of time. It's only two short blocks."

"To the station? I'd be very glad to drop you there." Good Samaritan J. Duff, he thought. But it was not quite so.

They got Bea in between them. She was hysterically silent, if there is such a thing, and kept clinging to the man's shoulder. Duff trotted out his ulterior motive, right away.

"I've got to go back to the Moriarity house," he said, "and the trouble is, I don't know the children. I wonder if you could tell me at least their names?"

"You want the kids' names?"

"Please, if you know them."

"Oh. I thought you must be a friend of Mary's. . . ."

"My name is Duff. I happened along in time to be of service. I'm not much more than a stranger. By the way, do you know a woman they call Brownie?"

"Yes . . . yes . . ." Walker said, rather cautiously.

"It seems that she died rather suddenly this afternoon."

"Brownie!" His voice squeaked with astonishment. The woman, Bea, slumped between them and paid no attention to what they were saying. "Not Brownie! What happend to her? She was a healthy old so-and-so. Excuse me."

"Mrs. Moriarity thinks poison happened to her."

"Holy . . . ! Look, turn down here. That's right. That's the station. Quaint, isn't it? Well, I'll *be!* Look, I'd like to do something to help Mary out, but you see

17

Only Look

t to get back. I work nights. Besides
home. What a mess, huh? Suicide?"

ow. Would you think so?"

y wouldn't. Brownie wouldn't want to die.
was alive, much. Didn't know what she was
mis.   So why die?"

"Oh?" said Duff. "And who was she?"

"Who? Why, she went to school with Mary. Maiden
lady, you see. Turns up every once in a while to visit.
Courtesy auntie to the children and all that. Old
acquaintance. Shouldn't be forgot."

Walker stopped talking, and his brown eyes looked
thoughtfully at the rain. Duff pulled up at the station.
His passengers made no move to get out, and he didn't
urge them.

"Tell me about the children," he prompted, "if you
have time."

"Oh, yes. Well. . . . Sit still, Bea, there's plenty of
time. Let's see, Paul's the oldest, must be fourteen or
fifteen. Then there are the twins, Diana and Alfred, a
couple of years younger. Then there's a girl in the
middle, that's Margaret. She'd be eleven or so. And
Rosamund, of course. And the baby's David. David's
. . . gosh . . . five, I suppose."

"Thank you very much," said Duff. "But Taffy?"

"That's Rosamund."

"And where," said Duff, surprising himself with a
question right out of his subconscious, "is Mr.
Moriarity?"

"I don't know," said Walker. "He hasn't been
around for quite a while."

"Five years?" Duff murmured.

"Mary's not a Catholic, either," Walker
looked embarrassed.

The woman said something. She said, "I feel sick."

"We'll get out. Little air. Cheer up, darling . . .
twenty minutes on the train, that's all. We'll take a cab
from 125th Street." But he stood in the open door a
moment, supporting her. Something was on his mind,
and he was hesitating.

"My name is MacDougal Duff," said the detective.

The man's face cleared. "Oh, yes," he said, "of
course. I see. Well, I'm glad to know it. Look, I don't
want to tell tales out of school, you know, and all that.
But if it was poison and it *wasn't* suicide . . ."

"Quite," said Duff dryly.

"Well, there's always Eve. Eve Norden. I don't
know, but there's been a feud there. Good old Brownie
did her dirt, a long time ago. There's something wrong
back in her family. Eve's family. Brownie knew. And
Eve's pretty near crazy, you know. If it was me, I'd . . .
uh . . . wonder. That's a tip, sir. And maybe it doesn't
mean a thing. You understand . . ."

"For God's sake!" said Bea, twisting angrily away.
"What is this! I'm sick, I tell you. I don't want to stand
around and gossip! What is this small-town routine? I
want to go home and pass out. I want to go home and
die!" She had the voice of a sophisticated shrew.

"All right. All right, honey. I'll get you home, and
you're not going to die."

"Now, listen . . ."

Exit, squabbling, thought Duff. He engaged his gear
and drove slowly away.

e Meredith. Too many Little Eva's
'I didn't mean to kill her," said Mary
it a lie those bare words could tell, if, for
y were written down. When he'd heard
the car, in the mood, he'd understood
pen᪥ . "I didn't mean that she should be killed."
That was the real sense of them. Mary had said
something, and she remembered it now. She had said
something about this Brownie, but she hadn't meant
her audience to assume that the woman needed killing.
It must have been something possible of this interpretation. Had somebody so interpreted it? Was
that Mary's trouble, that she must have given
somebody an idea?

Duff turned a page of his mind quickly. Unless it was
an accident. Oh, possible, for all he knew. Poison, by
accident. Not uncommon.

Yet he had a strong intuition that none of the people
he had met so far thought Brownie's death an accident.

CHAPTER 2

A city cop with a gimlet eye let him into the house. Much was being done there, in an efficient kind of bustle. Dr. Christenson, who stood in the hall while the tides of police activity flowed around him, introduced Duff to the county medical examiner, Dr. Surf, a good-looking man with an air of belligerence which turned out to be his playful way of being informal.

About to leave, he said. About to leave. Autopsy, of course. Oh, yes, samples of everything for the toxicologist. Not much doubt she died of poison. Well, get on with it. Dr. Surf would see everybody later. So glad to have met Mr. Duff, sir. He had a clipped kind of handshake. He said to Pring, evidently winding up a bit of gossip, "And if you catch up with our vanishing friend, they'll give you the county on a platter."

Pring said, "I'll bet. Ha ha." The coroner went away. Detective Pring was a leather-faced fellow, dark-

...ean. Detective Robin was, on the
...nd pink-fleshed. They were both
...MacDougal Duff. They turned to him
...less, Duff knew he was facing Rule
...in the detective's handbook: no unauth-
...son shall be permitted to view the body
or the ...ene of the crime.

So Duff told a whopper. "I'd better explain," he said
quietly, "that Mrs. Moriarity has retained me to look
into this business for her. She is upset, naturally. The
woman was her friend, and a death of this kind, in her
house . . ."

He made an effect. Robin beamed. "Say, that's fine.
I'd like to see you work, myself."

Pring shot him a dark and challenging glance.
"Sure," he said, "go ahead, if that's the way it is. Come
on in and take a look at her."

So Duff met the corpse.

Miss Emily Brown. Age, thirty-eight. Laid out on
the shabby red couch in the big colorful worn and
lived-in room at the left of the hall. He thought she
seemed older. Her unattractive face, ungilded by
cosmetics, was benign in death. A rugged nose. A long
chin. Black hair shot with gray. Cut off, mannishly. A
deep-bosomed, matronly body, tapering off with long
legs and large orthopedic shoes. Countesy auntie. Old
acquaintance. Never knew what she missed.

Duff said, "She didn't do it herself, doctor?"

"No, no," said Dr. Christenson. "I was here, you see.
Just leaving. No, she hadn't expected it. That was
obvious. Respiratory. Very quick. Must have been a
tremendous dose."

"Of what?"

The doctor shrugged. "I don't want to guess," he said.

"It was in the wine," said Pring dourly. Duff raised an eyebrow at him. "I think so," he went on. "She was O.K. She drank some wine. Five minutes later she was a goner. So I say it was in the wine."

"And you are probably quite right," Duff told him heartily. "No one else had any wine?"

"The girl says her mother did. But there was two bottles. It's a little bit balled up. I . . ."

Pring settled back on his stocky legs for a long story, but Duff stopped him.

"Don't bother now," he said. "I want to talk to the kids a minute. I'm going to stay here in the house. Mrs. Moriarity, of course, will be with her little girl in the hospital. Where *are* the children?"

"Upstairs," the doctor said. "And I've got to go! I— May I speak to you for a moment?"

Duff and the doctor went out into the hall. Dr. Christenson was tall and thick. He wore a narrow hedge of mustache over his wide mouth and rimless glasses with gold bows through which he peered anxiously with magnified eyes. He would be, Duff judged, about forty, perhaps a little more. A worried man.

"Mary wants you to . . . er . . . ?" The doctor had a way of not finishing his question.

Duff said, "Mary wants me to stay with the children."

"Did she really say . . . er . . . you're to work on this . . . er . . . ?"

"Perhaps that was my own idea," Duff admitted. "If it's my fee you are thinking about, don't. Sometimes I work for love."

"Well, I did . . . wonder." But the doctor was still dubious, still tentative, unconvinced and worried.

Duff drew his mouth down. "I'm in love," he announced. "I fell like—what is it they say?—a ton of bricks." His voice was cheerful. "Wonderful sensation."

"You fell in love?" The doctor looked very nervous indeed.

"Oh, yes. With Taffy, of course."

"With *Taffy!*" The doctor sighed. Then his mustache spread with a quick smile, and his eyes seemed relieved, at last. "I see. Yes, of course, I see. Well, I'm very glad . . . very glad. You will—er—watch everything here? I am glad."

"I'm glad you're glad," Duff murmured. The doctor's glances were conspiratorial, and Duff didn't know why.

"I must get out of here." Business with his watch again. "The kids are in the big room upstairs. Just knock. Introduce yourself. There's nothing grim about them. I'll try to get back. My—er—fiancee, a Miss Avery, may come along a little later. I've tried to reach her by phone, but I can't. Can't head her off. Don't know where she can be. So I want very much to be back before she—er—walks into this."

Duff said, "Please, before you go, tell me, who is Eve Norden?"

"Eve Meredith!" The doctor seemed astonished. "She's Mrs. Meredith now, of course. Lives next door. Where did you ever . . . ? How did you . . . ?"

24

"I have my methods," said Duff. "One more question. About Mr. Moriarity?"

"Mary divorced him," said Dr. Christenson bluntly.

"He is alive?"

"Oh, very much so. As far as I know. But what . . . ? But why . . . ?"

"You're in a hurry, aren't you?" Duff reminded him.

The doctor remembered that he was.

The stairs turned back on themselves at a square landing. Duff reached the upper hall and listened. Six white doors were closed and blank. The seventh was ajar, and there were voices behind it. He knocked gently.

Somebody sang out, "Come in."

The five Moriarity children made quite a crowd. This room was over the living room and just as large. There were twin beds. The walls were lined with shelves of books and toys and two long window seats. It looked a very pleasant place for small fry to live and play.

In one of the twin beds two small human animals sat side by side, hugging their knees under the covers, staring at him brightly. They were in their pajamas. The little boy had great big ears and great big dark-blue eyes. The little girl was as dark as a gypsy, with a black tangle of curly hair falling to the middle of her back, and pale, clear brown eyes. Tan eyes, Duff thought.

On the edge of the other bed sat an older girl, sedately. She was plump and tow-headed. Her hair was nearly pure white. Her eyes were dark. The effect was a little startling. Her middle front teeth were very wide and white. She said, "Yes?"

"My name is Duff. I'm the man who took your mother and your little sister to the hospital. I'm going to stay here tonight, in the house, if you don't mind. Your mother said to tell you *my* mother was one of the Mulligans."

All five faces dimpled and broke into understanding smiles. "Oh, my goodness," said the oldest girl.

"That's O.K., then," said the fat tow-headed boy on the window seat.

"How is Taffy?" said the other boy, the one who looked so much like Mary, with his long nose and very blue eyes.

"Taffy's going to be comfortable, I think. She's got a room all alone. Nobody in the other bed. And your mother is going to stay with her."

"That's good," they said. There was a wind of sighs.

"Let me see . . ." Duff looked around at them. "You're Diana?"

The oldest girl stood up, bent one round leg, and sat down again on her foot. "Well, I am, of course, but I don't see how you knew that. Don't tell me Mother gave you my right name! I didn't think she remembered what she named me."

"Sometimes she does when she's mad, Dinny," said the tow-headed boy calmly.

"Are you Alfred or Paul? Alfred, I should guess." The tow-headed ones would be the twins.

"That's right. He's Alfie. I'm Paul," said the boy who looked like Mary. "Can we go and see Taffy tomorrow, do you know?"

"I don't know," said Duff regretfully, "but we can find out. Let me get you all straight. That's David, I suppose."

The little fellow was embarrassed. He put his head down and squirmed. "Don't be like that, Davey," said the gypsy girl plaintively. "I'm Mitch."

"Well," said Duff, "there's only one person Mitch could be because there's only one unidentified child left. Therefore, you're Margaret."

They hooted. Alfred said, "Gee whiz, Mom musta been feeling formal. Say, there's a famous detective named Duff. Hey, Paul, you know who I mean?"

Paul nodded. Five pairs of eyes accused Duff hopefully.

"I am a detective," he admitted, feeling what little Davey must have felt. "MacDougal Duff."

"Mac Duff!" shouted Alfie. "Lay on, Mac Duff!" He put his hands on his thighs with a thump.

"Aw, shaddup," said Paul. "He doesn't like that. Who would, moron?"

"Oh, boy!" said Alfie. "Listen, are you going to figger out who bumped Aunt Brownie off?"

"Don't say that!" cried Dinny. "We don't know anything about it."

"Yes, we do," said Mitch. "She got poisoned."

"Well, all right, she's dead, isn't she?" Alfie, like his sister, had two front teeth that were broad and white, so that, with his plump pink face and white hair, he looked something like a jolly young albino walrus —except for those curious eyes, dark like Dinny's, and as startling under the pale and inconspicuous brows. "She's a *corpus delicti* now," he said.

Duff sat down on a toy chest. No, they weren't, as far as he could see, grim. They weren't scared, either. They didn't seem to think he was there to keep away the bogey man. In fact, Duff got the impression that any bogey man who showed up in this company would soon retire, a confused and frustrated fellow.

"As a matter of fact," he said, grinning, "I do intend to figger out what happened to Brownie, and I want you to help me."

"Oh, boy!" said Alfie. "Only we're starving."

"Oh, heavens, Alfie, we ate most of it," Dinny said. "Don't pay any attention to him, Mr. Duff. He's always starving."

"He doesn't look it," Duff said. "What's the matter? Oh . . . poison?"

"Dr. Norris said not to eat a thing, not to touch it, till they found out whether it was all right." Dinny's round face was serious but not alarmed.

"Dr. Norris?"

"Norris Christenson. We've known him forever."

"Well, I expect he was quite right, after all," said Duff. "Are you really hungry?"

"I am," Mitch said, bouncing in the most mysterious way, as if some force was lifting her up and down with no visible muscular effort on her part.

"I'm *hungry*," Davey said. "I on'y had some eggs."

"Right in the middle of supper," Alfie said. "Bingo."

Duff looked at the daylight. "It's not late. Your mother doesn't mind if you go out?" The boys looked insulted. "I don't know, you see," Duff soothed. "You'll have to tell me what the rules are. I was going to suggest that you two— Do you know a dogwagon? How about a mess of hamburgers?"

"Swell!" said Paul.

"Oh, wonderful!" said Dinny.

"Pickles, pickles, pickles," chanted Mitch.

"Ketchup," said Davey.

28

Duff looked at him doubtfully. "Is it all right?" he asked them. "I wouldn't want to feed you the wrong thing or do you out of your vitamins."

"We have hamburgers all the time," Mitch said. "We lo-ove them." She put on an ethereal look. Her thin dark face lighted and looked pure.

"My favorite fruit," said Davey, the five-year-old, with great finality.

All the other Moriarity kids howled with laughter.

"He's sumpin," Alfie said.

"He's a peanut," said Paul.

"One time at the beach I ate five hamburgers with ketchup on," said Davey. Nobody paid any attention to this remark, although Duff waited.

In the silence, then, he got out his wallet. "Well, suppose you—er—figger out your collected capacity and add on a couple for me."

"With pickles, I mean relish?" Alfie asked, his tongue stumbling over his ideas.

"Oh, I think with ketchup for me," Duff said. "Also, what do we want to drink?"

They were suddenly polite and quiet. It seemed to be up to him to suggest something.

"Milk? Ice cream soda? Pop? You don't drink coffee, I suppose. Or do you?"

Dinny said primly, "No, we don't. But we like malted milks very much, if that isn't too expensive."

"I don't suppose it's too expensive," Duff said gravely. "After all, we need our strength. Five dollars?"

Paul said, "Two eighty-five, if you want a malted, too. I guess coffee is only ten. That makes it two seventy-five?"

"Make mine coffee. Are you a lightning calculator?"

"He's scientific," Alfie said.

Paul cuffed at him. "Fifteen cents times eleven," he explained a little scornfully, "that's two hamburgers for everybody but Davey . . ."

"Waw!" said Davey.

"Well, you can't," said Dinny. "And Alfie's going to eat half of Mitch's second one. He always does."

"My eyes are bigger than my stomach," Mitch explained to the stranger complacently.

Duff stood up. His insides were bubbling with the desire to keep from laughing. "Does Davey expect five?" he asked a little anxiously.

"Oh, my goodness," said Dinny, "he never ate five hamburgers. Why, he hasn't got room!"

"He just thinks he did," said Paul pleasantly. "He gets ideas."

"I ate five hamburgers *an*' a hot dog," said Davey, "an' green ice cream an' I had a egg stomach."

"A what?"

"He means a stomach ache."

"Calm yourself, Davey," said Paul, "hold everything, bud."

"Well, suppose you boys come along," said Duff helplessly. "I'll get you past the policeman."

Pring and Robin and a man with a camera were in the hall near the front door as Duff and the boys came down.

"Yeah, but they've got no servants," Robin was saying. "Nobody here to visit. No callers, no company all day. So it's an inside job, if it *was* a job. That's all I say."

Pring said, "That may be. Somebody could get in. Place was wide open."

"Yeah, but, not empty. People around."

"If it was in the wine . . ." They heard Duff and his friends and were still.

Duff asked permission for the boys' errand, and it was granted. Pring, however, slipped his hands down over the young bodies and the pockets and gave them hard looks before he let them go. Paul looked back insolently. Alfie, however, submitted with a big grin of pure pleasure.

Then the boys were gone into the summer twilight.

Duff gathered around. The man with the camera slouched away. "This wine," Duff said, "where did it come from?"

"It was her own wine," Pring said. "Seems she bought it herself. The girl says she always had some around where she was, thought it was good for her. She bought a bottle yesterday, downtown, here. Had one glass earlier, and it was all right then."

"It stood open?"

"Yeah, in the pantry. But there's another bottle of the same brand. Some gone out of that, too. Don't know where it came from. Maybe Mrs. Moriarity bought it. We gotta go up to the hospital and see her."

"Could you possibly not bother her tonight? Little Taffy is quite sick, you know."

"Well . . ."

"I'm sure you can see her whenever you like, tomorrow. Then it was known that this wine belonged to Miss Brown? That she, alone, was likely to drink it? Is that the situation?"

"I guess it was, yeah."

31

"Then if somebody put something in the wine bottle or bottles, he was definitely after Miss Brown?"

"Sure. Or it could be. The girl says none of the rest of them liked it. Dubonnet. Tastes like medicine to her, she says."

"That makes it harder, doesn't it?"

Robin stopped chewing gum a moment and Pring said, "Huh?"

"I mean that it could have been done any time, all day. Or at least any time after the bottle was opened. Can't limit the opportunity."

"I don't know about that," Pring said. "It just so happens maybe we can. Also, we got fingerprints."

"Do you know whose?"

"Not yet. We'll have it by morning. We've got the bottles. We've got prints off of everybody . . . except Mrs. Moriarity."

Duff said, "Where were they all when it happened?"

"Having supper in the dining room. The kids and Miss Brown. Seems Mrs. Moriarity was upstairs with the sick little girl, and the doctor was up there with them. Says he came down, and Miss Brown, she got up from the table and spoke to him out here in the hall. Back there. By the stairs. Right by that radiator. Now, lessee . . . one of the boys was still out in the yard doing some work he wanted to finish. The other boy and the little one and the two girls—Well, wait. The big girl was in the kitchen a lot. She got supper, see. Anyhow, Miss Brown was drinking wine with her supper, and one of the bottles was right there on the table, by her place. She took her glass with her into the hall, and it was all right then, because she offered some to the doc, and he took a sip. She comes back to the table, and he

32

goes to the front door, see, gets his hat, he's leaving. She pours herself a full glass and gulps it and screams. Doc comes running back. In five minutes it's all over. I don't know what'll do that, but it did it."

"It was in the wine," Robin said. "Hadda be."

"Did you find any poison container?"

"Did we!"

"The place is full of poison," Robin said glumly. "Lousy with it. Cyanide, arsenic, nicotine, bichloride of mercury—what'll ya have?"

"Mrs. Moriarity has quite a garden," Pring explained. "She keeps all this stuff for killing bugs. Under lock and key in the stable out back."

"Yeah, but the key ain't under lock and key," said Robin, heaving at his own wit.

"That's so," Pring said. "She locks it up so nobody can get it by accident, but the key's hanging right there. A little bit high up, that's all."

Duff felt the feather edge of danger. A shiver whistled along his nerves.

"Has it been disturbed?" he asked.

"Don't know. Fingerprints. Tell you tomorrow."

"Good," he said. "When did Miss Brown arrive?"

"Friday night. She'd come and stay a week or ten days. Oh, two, three times a year. She had money, didn't have to work for a living. They say she traveled around a lot, winters in California. She's got a little apartment in New York, but she isn't . . . wasn't often there. She showed up Friday, late in the afternoon, and was going to stay till a week from today. Say, come and take a look at her stuff. She's gone, you know. Wagon came while you were upstairs. Let's go up, whadda ya say?"

"You're being darned co-operative," Duff said. "I hope I can do as much for you."

Pring grinned. His leathery face opened reluctantly, as if it hadn't grinned often. "You and us both," he said, "we hope. That wine bottle thing. I'm going home and write it down and kick it around awhile."

They took Duff up to a room at the back of the house, where Brownie had been accustomed to stay. It was a little bare, as if the Moriaritys had been too much in need of all the furniture they could find to spare much for the guest room. But it was a pleasant small bedroom, and Brownie's things were spread on the narrow single bed.

Her clothes. Sedate. Dark silks and dull prints. More health shoes. Her handkerchiefs and her toilet water. Her handbag. Checkbook, ration book, safe-deposit key, coin purse, hairpins, playing cards.

"She had this," Pring said. It was a snapshot, a very old one. The corners were smeared with something shiny. It was the picture of a baby sitting on a white cloth on the grass. There were flowers in a round bed behind it. The baby had a sad little face. It was swathed in clothing, although the time appeared to be summer. A bonnet with ruffles and ribbons, a beruffled coat of some sort, a white boot with tassels, embroidered skirts. The child was submerged. Babies are not dressed so any more. Even Duff knew as much. This picture was years old. And so, by now, was the baby.

"Doc Christenson says it's a picture of *him*," Pring told Duff. "Can you imagine? Said this Miss Brown got hold of it once and likes to kid him about it."

"She carried it with her?" Duff said curiously.

"Well, here it is." Pring threw it down with a shrug.

Duff studied it thoughtfully. There was no way, he reminded himself, of telling by that Victorian infant's getup whether the child in the picture was a boy or a girl. The hair was hidden by the bonnet. Besides, boys were as likely as girls to have long curls in those days. Duff sighed.

"And then there's this," Pring said. He put a newspaper clipping in Duff's hand. It was a headline only, the heading of a small item, type not very large, one column wide. It read: "Actor Burned in Car. Woman Companion Runs Away." That was all. No date. The paper was fairly white and crisp. Duff turned it over. On the other side was part of an advertisement for a preparation that concealed gray hair. It was the part that contained the address of the maker.

There was a clatter on the stairs.

"Ah," said Duff, "our hamburgers. Would you care to join us?"

"No," Pring said, "no, thanks. Uh . . . we're going to get out of here. We'll have to seal the dining room. If you wanna get in there tomorrow . . ."

"Of course," Duff said. "Thanks very much." He shook their hands.

"I won't leave anyone inside. But the man on the beat will keep an eye out. Just don't sample the food, eh?"

"We won't," Duff promised. "By the way, what do you know about Mr. Moriarity?"

"Oh," Pring, who had been poised to go, seemed to let his weight fall where he was. "Well, I dunno. He hasn't been living here."

"Not for years," Robin said.

"I just wondered. I don't see any head nor tail to this

thing yet, do you?" Duff was airy. "As a matter of fact, perhaps it was an accident."

They pulled their eyes from his face. "Well, we wish you luck on it," said Pring gloomily.

"Be seeing you."

"We'll lock up downstairs."

"Good night," said Duff.

CHAPTER 3

The kids hadn't opened the big paper bags yet when Duff came in. He felt that he had just missed hearing something said, and that they had meant him to miss it. They were not quite open. There was a little rustle of reserve in their greetings.

This didn't include Davey, who had gone to sleep. He looked, Duff thought, exactly like the Dormouse.

Duff opened the paper bags and dealt out one round of hamburgers. Mitch took charge of Davey's and began to pinch and poke at him. He woke up, presently, and seemed to pass without any transition at all from a state of sound sleep to a position well within the circumference of his hamburger.

Duff looked around and announced that he needed to ask all kinds of questions. He wondered if it would ruin their appetites to start now.

They said they didn't think so.

37

"What do we know, though?" Dinny wondered.

"Don't worry," said Alfie enthusiastically. "Whatever it is, he'll get it out of us."

"First, tell me about Brownie," Duff began. "What kind of person was she?" He relaxed on one of the window seats and bit into his hamburger, appearing, he hoped, in a mood for friendly gossip.

Dinny was curled up on the bed, leaning against the headboard. She wore a short dress of cotton plaid with big pockets in the skirt. Her saddle shoes had once been white. Her ankle socks were white and clean and pushed down in rumpled cuffs. She had fat, unshaped childish legs. Her hair was cut short and curled in a pale halo around her face, rippling at the temples like white silk. Her skin was not as miraculously clear as Taffy's, but it had the thin, fine texture that shows the blood through. Her air was grave and dignified. Every once in a while she licked her fingers as she ate, but she did it as a lady might. Her cheeks were too round and her mouth was lost, but her nose was straight and would someday, given a chance, be lovely.

"Oh, Brownie was all right," she said carelessly.

"She went to the same school as my mother," Paul explained.

"Practically in the family," Alfie said. "She was a spinster."

Duff looked at the girl and her two big brothers. Alfie was bigger than she, like a larger edition. So grownup they were, the three of them, talking to him, giving him obvious and superficial facts. And all the time thinking . . . what?

Duff realized that he wasn't going to cut under their facade without effort, or get behind the picture they

38

chose to give him of themselves. Young people, well-behaved, intelligent, interested, good bright children. He looked at their faces. Under a certain blandness, the intelligence was there and, he surmised, a whole world of keenly cbserved data, judged, weighed, synthesized by that intelligence and the fresh and unprejudiced approach of youth. Ah, yes, he thought, the grownups preach the sweetness and light, the rules and the proverbs, the shalt-nots and the platitudes . . . preach them to their young, although they themselves have never quite managed to live by them. And the children give back tit for tat. Amiably, they reflect the pattern. They pretend to be taken in. But they aren't, really. They reserve the right to draw other conclusions which they keep to themselves, and who can blame them?

He felt himself to be searching for a door into their secret world. He stalked, to change the metaphor, warily the prey of their confidence. And their real opinions.

"Did you like Brownie?" he said. "Was she pleasant to have around?"

Dinny shrugged.

"She brang us presents," volunteered small David.

"She did if you didn't ask for them," Dinny said a trifle scornfully. Duff raised his brows. He had a way of looking politely as if he didn't believe what he heard. It compelled Dinny to rush into explanation. "Once Mitch asked her what she'd brought, and she said 'nothing' and wouldn't give them to us. She was funny. She didn't want to be . . . oh . . . uh . . . I don't know . . ."

"She wanted to make out like it was a surprise," Alfie said.

"No," Dinny said, "that's not what I mean." She leaned back and gave up, as if she felt that no one would ever know what she had meant.

"She wanted to keep the initiative?" Duff suggested lightly.

"That's right!" said Dinny, sitting up again and looking surprised. "*She* wanted to be the one to give out stuff. And get a kick out of it. But if we just assumed she was always going to bring us presents, then she *had* to do it. She liked to make us wait and wonder. Sometimes she'd treat us and sometimes she wouldn't." Dinny's dark eyes looked at Duff straight, and she paid him the compliment of not talking down. "She was whimsical about it," Dinny said, "because then it made her feel powerful."

"I see," Duff saw. He also felt a little shock.

"She was darned nasty to Taffy once," Paul said in his man's voice, gruff and truculent.

"What . . . ?" said Dinny.

"Oh, yeah, that picture thing," said Alfie. "Yeah . . ."

"Taffy's always drawing pictures," Paul explained. Speech came from him reluctantly. He was not as glib as the twins. "She just likes to. Well, she drew a picture of Brownie, the last time Brownie was here and wrote on it something about a witch." Paul was in a straight chair which he tipped back, maintaining his balance with the muscles of his strong young thighs. He had on a pair of cotton trousers and a blue shirt, open at the neck. His substantial feet were in sneakers, his tanned ankles bare. He was a good-looking boy, especially if a smile lit his face. In repose, it fell into rather a glum expression, which glumness was apparent now.

"Oh, I remember!" Mitch bounced. " 'Brownie is a witch.' That's what she wrote."

"Boy, was *she* mad!" Alfie said in his joyful bumbling way. Sometimes he just missed a stutter. "She hit the ceiling, didn't she?"

"Taffy didn't mean anything," Dinny said.

Paul looked at Duff's eyebrow and away. "Taffy's funny," he said. "She gets a streak on something. Asks questions and talks about it all the time until she knows everything she can find out about it. And then she'll start asking about something else. Well, she was on witches. It was around Halloween, and she got started on witches. You see, my mother thought she'd scare herself too much. Anyhow, Mom had been trying to tell her all about *good* witches."

"Like in *Oz*," cried Mitch. Mitch's contributions were all little cries, yet she was curiously self-contained.

"That's right," Dinny said. "Of course, Taffy didn't mean to insult anybody." Her face looked grieved.

"Old Brownie didn't even bother to try and find out what Taffy was thinking about," said Paul angrily. "She just tore up the picture and made Taffy cry."

"Yeah, that was mean," Alfie agreed. Alfie's fat feet in sloppy moccasins massaged each other.

Duff thought to himself that the Moriaritys stood together. Injure one and you injured them all.

He said carefully to Paul, "Brownie wasn't the type to put herself in Taffy's place, then?"

"Or anybody's," said Paul bluntly.

"No sympathetic imagination?"

"No," said Paul, responding with sudden maturity. "She just blundered along, hit or miss, being herself."

"I see," said Duff gratefully. Paul, embarrassed, shifted in his chair and threw his arm over the back of it.

"What's Taffy interested in now?" Duff asked them.

"What . . . ?" said Alfie, turning to his brother as if Paul would be sure to know.

But Dinny answered. "Nurses. All about nursing. That's because Aunt Eve goes up to the hospital to be a nurse's aid. I mean, that's how Taffy got started."

"Gee, Taffy's going to have a wonderful time in the hospital," Paul said, looking boyish and happy.

"I'd like to get the whole sequence of the last few days," said Duff. "Dinny, you start. Tell me when she came, when you first heard she was coming, what happened, and so forth."

"Mother got a letter a week ago," Dinny said promptly. "Brownie was in California all spring. The letter came from some place on her way east. It said she was coming Friday, and she did, late in the afternoon, and we had supper, and she and Mother got up to date on the news. We didn't do anything after supper, did we?"

The boys shook their heads.

"Well, Saturday morning she hung around watching Mother and me do the chores. And we had lunch. After lunch I went to the beach, so I don't—"

"For one thing, she went downtown with Mother," Alfie said.

"That's right, because she got the wine."

"The wine," murmured Duff. "She always had a bottle of that particular brand, I understand."

"Oh, yes. Mother forgot, this time. We usually manage to have some all ready for her."

"Nobody else drinks it?"

"Well, not usually. Sometimes. Nobody in this family. But she doesn't offer it. She doesn't look upon it as a social drink," said Dinny. "She looks upon it as a tonic."

"Oh?"

"That's the way she *talked*," said Dinny, "but *I* think . . ."

"Yes?"

"I think she liked to get a little bit high. I don't know whether she knew it or not."

"She sure did guzzle it, didn't she?" Alfie said. Alfie was sitting on the window seat, leaning forward, eager and alert. His two and a half hamburgers had long since vanished. His white hair stood up like a ruff at the back. For all his air of being comical and puppyish and impulsively clumsy, Duff felt that those dark eyes in that round pink face belonged to some wiser and older soul, and that they watched, missing nothing.

"Shaddup, Alf. One at a time," said Paul, the orderly mind.

"O.K., O.K.," croaked Alfie.

"When was the wine opened? Not Saturday?"

"No," Dinny answered, "because Mr. and Mrs. Miller came over Saturday night and they played bridge and had Tom Collinses. She didn't need any excuse to drink a little."

"Then it wasn't opened until . . . ?"

"This afternoon, I guess."

"What happened today?"

"Well, Sunday morning, as usual. We had a late breakfast and read the papers. Mother worked in the garden, as usual. We didn't have a real lunch, just a

43

snack because breakfast was so late, and besides it was bacon and eggs. And then we were all off somewhere. I mean, I went to the beach again with Jean. And the boys went, too, didn't you? And Mitch was over at a friend's house. None of us kids were home but Taffy and Davey."

Davey was, by now, asleep again with ketchup on his chin.

"Go on," Duff said.

"I got home about a quarter of five, because I had to get supper. Taffy had been taken sick. I don't know just when. Sometime in the afternoon. Mother was upstairs with her. Poor kitten, she whoopsed all over the place. Brownie was sitting out on the terrace when I came through the back way, and she told me. She had the wine open because she was drinking some."

"At a quarter of five?"

"Yes."

"Alone?"

"Yes."

"Go on."

"Well, I got dressed. You see, we walk down to the beach in our bathing suits from here. And hung out my suit and started to boil some eggs and fix a salad."

"You were in the kitchen?"

"Yes, I was getting supper from about five until we sat down. But we didn't sit down until six-thirty, I guess. The doctor came. The boys got home, and Mitch—"

"Times, please."

"Well, let's see. The doctor came about six to look at Taffy. The boys were home by five-thirty."

"I had to spray the roses," Paul said. "Mom told me to."

"Paul helps a lot in the garden," Dinny explained. "He mows the lawn."

"I got home around six," said Mitch brightly. "I know because Sally's mother *sent* me home."

"What," asked Duff, "was Brownie doing all this time? Still sitting on the terrace, drinking wine?"

"Oh, no. I heard her go upstairs pretty soon after the doctor came. I guess she wanted to see what he had to say about Taffy. She came down—oh, a little before six-thirty—and said Mother said we should go ahead with supper. And we all sat down—"

"Except Paul," Alfie reminded her.

"That's right. Paul was still working in the rose garden."

"You have to use up all the spray," Paul explained. "Once you get the sprayer full, you just keep going until it's empty."

"You kept going until when?"

"Until Alfie called me," Paul said. "I'd just about finished. I was going to clean the sprayer after supper. I opened it to let the pressure out."

"Had it begun to rain?" Duff looked politely skeptical about this whole yarn, and Paul responded.

"Sure. It was raining a little."

"You continued to spray the roses in the rain?"

"I told you, you've got to get that stuff all out of the sprayer. Besides, it was a contact spray." Duff said nothing. "Look," Paul said, "some kinds of bugs chew up the leaves. So you put a stomach poison like lead arsenate on the leaves, and they eat it and die. But some of them have beaks, like, and they suck. You have to get them by a contact poison. Hit them with it. Makes them suffocate. Well, naturally, if you're trying to coat the leaves and it rains, the rain will wash it all off. But if you're trying to kill a bug by hitting him with the stuff . . ."

"He's dead!" said Alfie. "Let it rain."

"Thank you," said Duff. "I think I understand now." He turned to Dinny. "You sat down at the table about six-thirty? All the rest of you?"

"That's right. I was up and down, though, bringing in stuff. We had deviled eggs and a green salad and cheese spread and jelly and peanut butter and toast and—"

"Pickles," said Mitch drowsily.

"Yeah, and what? Fruit. That's all."

"You mean we were going to have it," Alfie said.

"Brownie was eating with us. We heard the doctor come down and make a call on the phone."

"Time?"

"I don't know. Close to six-thirty."

"Brownie got up and went out into the hall?"

"Yes, to talk to him."

"Were they in your view?"

"Not while I was in the dining room," said Dinny. "My back was turned."

"Any of you?"

"I could see them, kind of," said Alfie.

"Did you see the doctor drink out of her wine glass?"

"No. Because I . . ."

"Oh, I saw that," Dinny said. "You see, I took Mother a tray, upstairs. I just waited for the toast. I went right by where they were . . . and he did take a sip. She said something like he looked as if he needed it, and he took a sip, just kidding, you know."

"It was not poisoned at that time," Duff said. "How long did they talk?"

Dinny said, "You'll have to ask somebody else this part. I took Mother's tray up and was just coming down again when she screamed. And the doctor told me to get Mitch and Davey upstairs as fast as I could, so that's what I did."

"Wait," Duff said. "What about the second bottle of wine?"

"I don't know," said Dinny with a furrowed brow. "It was standing in the pantry when I got home from the beach. Both bottles were. Both had been opened, and both had some gone. Brownie had a glass out on the terrace. I don't know why she'd have opened them both. Or where the second one came from, because only one was standing in the pantry the night before. Or this morning. I don't understand about that second bottle."

"At supper, did you put a bottle in the dining room for her?"

"No, I didn't. She put it on herself, when she came down. She just took a bottle. Which one, I wouldn't know. They were just alike, anyway."

"Then you didn't touch it?"

"No, but I touched the other bottle. The one left in the pantry. I poured a glass for Mother."

"Look here, my dear, did your mother drink it?"

"Yes, she did," said Dinny. "Anyhow, it's gone from the tray. Why?"

"We have Bottle A," Duff said, "which Brownie

herself took to the dining room and which stood on the table there. Bottle A was not poisoned at, say, six-thirty, because the doctor, who remains healthy, took a sip that had been poured from it. Now, according to you, Bottle B was not poisoned, either. Where is that tray now?"

"They took it. They took everything with any food. But I noticed the wine was gone. She'd started to eat. The toast was b-bitten . . ."

Duff smiled at her and broke the spiral of mounting tension. "We've got to get all these tiny details clear, you know. Now, let's see. What time do you think you poured the wine from that bottle?"

"Well, I don't know. But it was only a few minutes after we sat down. I only waited to toast a piece of bread. Then I got up and took the tray. It was just about when Brownie went out in the hall. Alfie, don't you remember?"

"Yeah, but you were worrying about Paul, and I went out and yelled for him."

"Go slow," said Duff. "This is getting complicated. Now, we have a bottle of wine on the table. Not poisonous yet. Dinny goes to the kitchen and then upstairs?" She nodded. "Alfie goes where?"

"To the back porch."

"And Brownie goes out into the hall." Duff contemplated this arrangement of people. "Now, when she came back— How much later?"

"I was just getting back, too," said Alfie. "Couple of minutes, that's all."

"And she refilled her glass?"

"Yeah."

"She drank it?"

"Yeah. It seemed to hurt her mouth and throat," Alfie said. "And then she . . . you know."

"O.K." Duff stopped him. "It would seem that in two or three minutes, there, the wine which had been harmless became fatal. Is this where we are getting? If, of course, it *was* the wine. Now, who remained in the dining room with Bottle A?"

"Mitch and Davey," Dinny said, sucking her breath in.

Mitch twisted down under the covers. "I didn't either!" she said indignantly. Her small face was nearly hidden.

"You didn't what? Come on, Mitch," Alfie coaxed her, "you might as well say."

"I didn't stay there. I went out in the kitchen."

"What for?" demanded Paul.

"Never mind," Mitch's voice was smothered and she bounced a little.

"Leaving Davey?" Duff said gently.

They looked at the little sleeping boy. "Oh, my gosh," said Dinny. "You'll never get out of him what happened. He makes things up. He's liable to tell you it was a lion or an elephant. Mother says he doesn't know the difference yet between what he makes up and what really happens."

"Yeah, he'll say anything," confirmed Alfie.

Mitch heaved.

"Still," mused Duff, "have we pinned this down to the crucial two or three minutes? We do not, in the first place, know that the poison was in the wine, although it seems, on the face of things, to have been there.

However, neither do we know—or do we?—whether she poured herself that first glass out of Bottle A or Bottle B. Who saw her?"

They looked blank.

"Perhaps she poured a glass in the pantry and carried the bottle in as an afterthought. The *other* bottle."

"I get it," said Paul. "All the nonpoisoned wine came out of Bottle B. And the poison was in Bottle A all the time."

"It must have been," said Dinny with a little sigh.

"No, it wasn't either!" Mitch sat up and her curls wagged. "Because if it was, why isn't Davey dead, then?"

"Davey?"

"I wasn't going to tell on him. But he took some of that wine while Brownie and everybody was gone. Oh, Davey lo-oves wine. He did. He was bad. I know he isn't supposed to. But he drank it. 'Course he spilled some. I took his glass away and went out in the kitchen and washed it. That's what I went out there for. I scolded him, Dinny. But there wasn't any sense," said Mitch shrewdly, "in getting Brownie mad at him. So that's why I did it."

"Ye Gods," said Alfie.

"Did you tell this to the detectives? The men who were here?"

"*They* didn't talk to *me*. They just talked to Dinny and Paul. But they took my fingerprints."

"Oh, gosh, Mitch, now everything's mixed up again."

"Well, I can't help it." Mitch bounced.

"*If* it was the wine," Duff sighed. "I'm beginning to

wonder. Now, let's go over it again. A few minutes after six-thirty, Brownie went into the hall carrying with her a glass of wine. She offered some to the doctor. We know it was not poisoned. Bottle A stands on the table in the dining room. Bottle B stands in the pantry. Since Davey samples Bottle A, we know it is not yet poisoned. Since Dinny takes some from Bottle B to her mother upstairs, we know Bottle B is not yet poisoned.

"Where were each of you? Tell me again."

"I went upstairs," said Dinny, "with the tray. I didn't get down again until just as she screamed."

"I was working outside," said Paul. "Alfie yelled, and I put the sprayer down and loosened the top and came in to wash my hands. I was in the kitchen when she screamed."

Alfie said, "I went through the French doors, out on the back porch, and over to the corner and yelled. Paul yelled, 'O.K.' So I came in again. I got back to the table just when she did. Brownie, I mean. She was putting more wine in her glass."

Duff turned to Mitch, who had come out of the covers as a snail will come out of his shell when nobody's looking. Mitch was small for her age, very tiny, and thin, too, compact with energy. Her eyes were brilliant and too pale a brown in her sunbrowned face, as if they caught the light. She tossed her curls. "I told you. Everybody went away, and Davey grabbed the wine. So I scolded him and took the glass out and washed it."

"Did you take the bottle, too?" Duff asked softly. "Did you happen to swap those bottles?"

"Oh, Mitch . . ." said Dinny reproachfully.

"I never did any such a thing!" snapped Mitch and disappeared with a great heave of the blankets.

Duff raised his eyebrows at the others.

Paul shook his head, biting his lip, looking grave. His long nose seemed to lengthen with sober thought. Alfie shrugged and rolled his eyes. Dinny sighed.

Duff said, "Well, let's suppose Bottle B was poisoned. Bottle A was not. Suppose, while only Davey sat there, the bottles were changed by someone."

"But Mother . . ." Dinny cried.

"I know," Duff said. "Was it your idea to take her some wine?"

"I thought she'd be tired." Dinny looked for a moment like a plump puzzled angel, her white halo poised, head thrown back.

"But if she didn't really want it? Perhaps she only pretended to drink it, to please you. Perhaps she didn't drink it, after all."

"We can ask her," said Paul with dryness and precision, as one who reminds the rest of a world of fact.

"But you're saying"—Dinny's hair seemed to rise, somehow, and stand on end—"you're saying I nearly poisoned my mother!"

Duff said, gently, "We are doing a lot of wild speculating without any facts. Tomorrow, we'll know better."

A telephone rang.

Dinny said, "But Mother . . ."

"I'll go," Duff said, "if you please." So Alfie showed him the upstairs phone, in Mary's room, across the hall.

It rang again. Duff picked it up.

"Yes?"

52

"Professor Moriarity?"

"WHAT!"

"I beg your pardon. Is the doctor theah?" said the voice with definitely British inflections.

"Do you mean Dr. Christenson?"

"Yes, yes, of course."

"No, he is not here, but he may be back." Duff had recovered himself and he purred. "Can I give him a message?"

"Tell him that Oliver O'Leary would like to speak with him. *Do* you mind?"

"Not atawl," returned Duff in the same rat-a-tat.

"Thenk you. Sorry to trouble you." Click.

Duff put his long fingers through his hair.

He looked around the pleasant, shabby room, saw Mary's tumbled desk, her modest dressing table, her slippers on the floor. The room had a sweet smell. A woman's room. Duff found himself staring at her slippers. They seemed to him to be very small and dainty.

He realized with some surprise that he did not at all relish the idea of questioning the Moriarity kids about their father.

CHAPTER 4

"Hey, the doorbell's ringing." Alfie's head came around the door. "You want me to go? Is there anybody downstairs?"

"Maybe it's Constance Avery," Dinny said. "She was supposed to come over." Paul leaned on the doorjamb behind her, saying nothing.

Duff looked at his watch. It was a few minutes after nine. "I'll go down. After all," he muttered, "I am the official discourager of bogey men around here." They let him through the little crowd the three of them made at Mary's door. As he started down the stairs Duff had a clear intuition that as soon as he had gone, they were going to say some things to each other that they didn't want him to hear.

So convinced was he that he paused on the landing, out of their sight, and deliberately listened.

Mumble, mumble, hush. Then a fierce whisper. "But he'll think Davey did it!" *Ssh . . . mumble . . .* silence.

The doorbell was playing "Shave and a haircut, bay rum." Duff went on down.

At the door there was a slim, sad fellow of indeterminate age whose brown eyes fixed themselves on Duff's face with an appeal both desperate and comical. "MacDougal Duff?" His manner was almost a burlesque of delicate formality. The eyes rolled. "Name of Haggerty. Few moments of your valuable time? May I come in?"

"What do you want?" Duff asked him pleasantly.

"Mr. Duff," Haggerty said in something like a confidential whisper, "you can do me a great favor. It so happens, unfortunately, I am out of a job."

"Indeed?" Duff drew back a little, amused. The man stepped in. He turned his toes out as he did so, making a leg, so that his movement was formal, like part of a bow, and yet there was a certain springiness and alacrity that was comical, too.

"I won't bore you with the details, Mr. Duff. But I was a news reporter. Last week they threw me out."

"Unjustly," murmured Duff.

Haggerty nibbled on his lip. His eyes were wells of sadness. "That may be," he said. "What's past is past. The future concerns me. *Now*, it is up to me to make good. I've got to redeem myself." He threw out his hand, moving the arm from the elbow. "I've got to prove they were wrong. For instance"—the voice softened down—"here is a death, mysterious. Murder, because"—here the eyes flew open wide to punctuate—"the famous MacDougal Duff is quietly investigating."

Duff pursed his lips.

"Wait." Haggerty seemed to sense Duff's impulse to

throw him out, too. "If I can get the inside track here, if I can scoop the story, why then—then! I can make them eat their words."

The man was unbelievable. He spoke in a series of cliches. He could easily have been making fun. Yet the impression he gave was of total naivete. The pan was dead, somehow. He let through no flavor of sarcasm.

"I don't quite understand why *I* should be expected to do you a favor," Duff said, reasonably. He heard the kids on the stairs behind him. Some of them had come down into the hall.

"You haven't got anything against me, have you?" Haggerty said. "It may so happen, I can tell you some things you don't—er—know." He was arch and sly and dead serious all at once.

"Can you?" said Duff indifferently.

"Let me give you a sample. For instance"—Haggerty sank his voice—"did you know that Miss Emily Brown, the dead woman, held the mortgage on this property?"

The statement, spoken as in a melodrama, seemed to bounce and echo off the walls. Behind him, Duff could feel the kids being as quiet as mice. He laughed. "Well! Was she about to foreclose, do you think? Have we here the motive?"

Haggerty's melancholy eyes remained fixed. "So it was murder," he said morosely. "I thought so." He actually took out of his pocket a notebook and a pencil. Furthermore, it was a stub pencil, and he licked it.

Duff said, "I'm sorry, Mr. Haggerty." He had a formal manner of his own, and it was not comical. It was ice.

Haggerty started backward, shuffling his feet. "By

the way," he said with the air of pulling out a desperate plum, "there's an escaped convict around somewhere. Did you know . . . ?"

"Oh, thank you," said Duff sweetly. "I'm glad to know that. Thank you very much."

"O.K.," said Haggerty, "Just as you like, sir. But I don't give up. I warn you." His feet scrambled for the doorstep.

"Just don't fall," Duff said kindly. He began to swing the door shut. Haggerty let the screen door back behind him. Duff saw the man look up and rub his face as if he'd struck a cobweb, a queer frightened gesture.

Dinny was hanging on the newel post, and Davey, like a little barnacle, clung to her behind. She giggled faintly, perhaps nervously. Mitch stood a step higher, very quiet, not giggling.

"Was he really a reporter?" demanded Alfie. "Gee, is this going to be in the papers?"

Duff surveyed his fat innocence glumly. "That," he said, "was such an incredibly bad imitation of a reporter that I am almost compelled to believe that the creature *is* a reporter." He watched their faces. "Is that true, about the mortgage?"

"What mortgage?" Paul was coming down the stairs.

"Did Brownie . . . ?"

"Oh. Oh sure." Paul caught the question before it was all asked, as if the point had been close to the surface in his mind. "Who was that at the door?" He didn't wait for an answer but went to the front door with a marching step, opened it, pushed open the screen, and looked out.

Being the man of the house, Duff thought.

"Davey says his ear aches," said Dinny in an anxious

57

voice. "Maybe it does, and maybe it doesn't." She sighed. "I don't *think* he's got a temperature."

"Naw, he hasn't," said Mitch, touching Davey's brow with the air of a wise little old woman.

Paul said gruffly, over his shoulder, "He's probably faking."

"He's an awful faker," agreed Alfie.

Duff looked down at Davey, whose small tanned face was now contorted to indicate pain, although he made no sound or moan except to suck in his breath in a kind of audible wince.

Alfie sauntered into the room where the piano was and began to drum out, "Up we go—into the wild blue yonder—," with one bold finger.

"Tell Alfie not to play the piano," said Davey in dying tones. "I don't feel well."

"Ask him which ear, and I'll get the mince candy," said Mitch briskly.

MacDougal Duff felt perfectly helpless.

At that moment, loud and clear, from upstairs came the embarrassing sound of a flushing toilet.

Duff checked in a flash. Paul, standing in the door. Alfie in the arch. Mitch and Davey and Dinny here at the foot of the stairs. Five Moriaritys.

He saw Dinny's plump body become very still and stiff. Her dark eyes turned warily, but she kept talking without a break, telling him smoothly, her voice a little light, but steady, that one asked Davey which ear in order to check, later, and that if he wouldn't eat chocolate thin mints, he was probably sick.

Paul came down the hall toward them. His face was red. Alfie took his hands out of his pockets and thrust them in again. "Well, get them, why don't you?" he exploded.

Mitch perched like a frozen butterfly on the edge of a step. She didn't seem to be breathing.

Duff said quietly, "Who's upstairs?"

Dinny said, "What?" with a little start and looked at him wide-eyed.

So Duff brushed by and went up quickly, with Alfie on his heels. "What's the matter? What do you mean?"

"You heard what I heard," said Duff skeptically.

"No, I didn't. I didn't hear anything." Alfie faltered and hung back.

There was no one on the second floor, although the toilet in the front bathroom was just subsiding.

Duff went up to the third floor, and there was no one there either. As far as he could tell, alone.

He came slowly down, and on the second level the Moriaritys flocked around him. A chocolate-coated Davey was pronounced a cure and dumped into bed. Dinny kept saying, "That's awfully funny. I don't understand it. Are you sure you heard anything?" Mitch said she was scared, but she looked excited. The boys watched Duff's face.

He considered the layout of the Moriarity house. On the second floor there was Mary's room at the front, over the little music room downstairs, then the bath, then, squeezed into a corner, a tiny room that belonged to Davey. The big bedroom over the living room, they told him, was normally inhabited by Mitch and Taffy.

The hall led back, then, and turned to end in another bath. Dinny's room was on the southeast corner, over the dining room. The guest room, where Brownie had stayed, was next, over the kitchen. There were back stairs leading down at the very back of the house and, oddly, they went down from Brownie's room and went

59

up, too. Dinny told him that this arrangement had often distressed their mother. "Mother wants to tear them out and have a breakfast room downstairs, but she can't afford to, and anyhow, not now, with the war . . ."

"It must be handy for the boys," Duff remarked.

"Oh, it is," they said heartily and then caught each other's eye a little sheepishly.

Paul and Alfie had the whole back wing of the house, up on the third floor. A paradise for boys, it was, with the eaves coming down to built-in cupboards and seats and shelves. Dormer windows. A whole laboratory in a corner. Three model airplanes zooming off the ceiling on wires. Stolen signs. One bed advised visitors to keep off the grass. On the door of their bath it said, "Please do not talk to the motorman."

There was a small uninhabited maid's room up there, in the front. And three small storerooms along the side of the house opposite the stairs. Not much in them—garment bags, an old rocker, boxes and books and trunks.

All this Duff had seen, and nothing seemed significant except that it was a maze. The whole house, at least the two top floors, was peppered with doors. On the third floor there was a way from each room into the next room and from each room into the hall. Therefore, one might run circles or figure-eights or any other funny figures around about and in and out. The second floor was much like it. No dead ends. There was simply no way to be sure that somebody was not always one lap ahead of you in this house unless you had a whole corps of trusted helpers, or dead silence and the ears of a lynx.

Furthermore, the circles went in three dimensions. There were the back stairs and the front stairs. There was even a laundry chute all the way up, although it was too narrow for a man's shoulders. There might, Duff thought, for all he knew, be two or three ways down outside, by way of roof and gutter, or rope and vine, and if so the boys were the ones to know it.

Oh, no doubt. No doubt at all. If these kids wanted to hide someone here, in their big old house, it was quite possible for them to do so.

Postulate a person hidden in the house. Consider the strategic position of the back stairs, coming down into the kitchen, as they did, at the back. Look at these clever Moriarity kids and remember their solidarity. Ask himself whom they would hide?

Duff asked himself and told himself the answer.

He led his troop down to the first floor. The big house echoed and creaked. Was it empty, above them, except for Davey in his bed? Or was there a hidden person? Someone to whom these kids were bound to be loyal?

And, if not, who had flushed the toilet while everyone known to be in the house had been on the first floor, under Duff's eye?

With the kids following after, as if he had been the Pied Piper, Duff stalked the downstairs hall and peered about. The music room, the big living room, the dining-room door, glass-paned and locked, at the end of the main hall, facing the front door. The cross hall, back here, ended at his left in a garden door that led to the terrace, and it was locked. At his right the same hall led to a "backdoor," opening to the driveway on the west, and that was locked, too. The cellar door was under the stairs, and locked. The kitchen, on the southwest, with the back stairs coming down, was in a state of quiet confusion. The pantry stole a little space from both dining room and kitchen and lay between them at the back of the house. It was locked up from the kitchen side.

They couldn't see into the dining room through the glass hall door, now that it was dark.

"Tell me, please," Duff said, "what happened after Brownie screamed?"

"They took her in the living room," said Alfie. "The doctor did."

"I got the kids, and we went up to Taffy's room, and Mother came down," said Dinny breathlessly.

Paul said, "They chased Alfie and me outside, after a while, so I thought I might as well clean the sprayer." He eyed Duff as if he challenged him to find this unreasonable. It didn't sound unreasonable. It sounded like one of Paul's facts.

Duff pursued his line of inquiry, reaching his point.

"No one stayed in the dining room?"

"No. The doctor said not to touch any food. He said that right away. We stayed out of there."

"Nobody was *in* the dining room," Alfie said, "because I hung around on the back porch, and I'd have heard them. Why? What's the idea? I don't see . . . ?"

"Is your toaster automatic?"

They shook their heads.

"I wonder who turned it off? Did any of you?"

"Oh, Lord, maybe it's still on!"

"If it was, we could see it," Paul said, peering close to the glass. "It gets red. No, it's off, all right."

"The detectives must have done it," said Alfie, "for gosh sakes."

"We must ask," Duff purred.

He went back to the living room and sat down. He thought: According to witnesses, she died about six-forty to six-forty-five. Therefore, a matter of minutes before the rain began to come down so hard. He said aloud, "Where were all of you in that heavy rain?"

"I was upstairs," Dinny said, "with Taffy and Mitch and Davey."

"I was in the stable," Paul said, "putting the sprayer away. I got caught out there."

"I was on the back porch," said Alfie. "Holy cats, did it rain!"

"You still think you'd have heard someone in the dining room?"

Alfie considered. "Yes, I would. It was kind of hollow."

Duff recognized the truth of that observation.

"But she was dead," Paul said patiently.

"Yes. Yes, she was. And we don't seem to be able to tell very much about it, do we?" Duff smiled at them. "Perhaps we'll know more tomorrow. Let's talk about something else." He appeared to relax. "What do you want to be when you grow up, Dinny?"

"An actress!" She reacted promptly, with no hesitation whatsoever. There she stood, fat and certain, and Duff felt dismay, and, in a moment, wonder.

"I'm going to be a dancer!" cried Mitch, swinging out a thin limber leg. Duff suddenly saw Mitch in tarleton with a spotlight on her.

"You go right straight to bed!" Dinny turned on Mitch in a fury. "Go on, now. Hop it. Mother'd have a fit. You go to bed and go to sleep. Hurry up."

Was it fury or flurry? Duff wondered. Because he'd caught her off guard, this young Dinny who wanted to be an actress. She ought not to have confessed that, because she had, he knew now with intuitive certainty, been acting for hours.

He knew he was going to have to ask that other question, sometime, whatever his reluctance. The impulse—and later he wondered if it had been telepathic—came to him to ask it now.

"Tell me," he drawled, "was your father a professor?"

"Huh! Gosh, no!" cried Alfie and was obviously struck silent by a thought.

Dinny was in the arch with Mitch, but they waited and listened.

"My father was an actor," Paul said quietly.

They were all very still for a moment. Duff, too. Dinny moved, as if to drag herself from a dream.

But Alfie bubbled over. "Say, listen, *we* oughta be on the other side!" he crowed. "You know? *Our* name is Moriarity! Isn't it? Gee, whiz, don't you know who Professor Moriarity *was!*"

"Shaddup!" said Paul.

CHAPTER 5

Enter Constance Avery. Duff went to the door and there she was at last, a tall young woman in a butter-colored linen suit, the color of her hair. She had a long oval face and a well-kept complexion that was like a mask. She wore no hat, and her fair hair was pulled flat from a center part, which gave her a look of being out of fashion. However, she did not seem behind the mode, but ahead of it, as if by tomorrow everyone would look just like her. She stood tall. Her suit was exquisitely tailored, her feet and ankles slim, her stocking seams precise, her white gloves pure white.

She pronounced her name so as to make Duff feel that he was expected to know who this was. He bowed, ever so slightly. "Please come in, Miss Avery. My name is Duff. Dr. Christenson asked me to say that he would be back. He had hoped to return before you came. Mrs. Moriarity isn't here, I'm sorry. She is at the hospital with her little girl."

"Oh dear!" said Miss Avery with exactly the proper accent of alarm.

She smiled at the boys. Alfie grinned back, with his tusks out, and Paul shifted his feet. She walked gracefully into the living room and, not knowing what had lain there so recently, sat down on the red couch. She crossed her ankles, not her knees, and began to pull off one white glove with delicate care.

Her eyes were gray, and there was not quite enough color in her brows and lashes to set them off. They seemed a little cold, and there was something faintly haughty in the way the fine skin drew up above them.

"Dr. Christenson," purred Duff, "has been trying to reach you, I know."

"Has he really?" she said. "But of course . . . I was repairing the henhouse."

Intrigued by this extraordinary statement, Duff nevertheless hid his surprise and offered a cigarette. They went through the graceful little ceremony of lighting it. Duff noticed her hands. They were smooth enough, yet he could tell that the skin on their backs was not elastic any more. Her long nails wore immaculate pink polish. Duff went to a chair opposite, concluding from this evidence that she was older than she looked and that whatever she meant by repairing a henhouse, those hands had not done it.

"I haven't met you before," she said. Her eyes had been summing Duff up, his lanky elegance, his quiet manner, the authority of his personality. She was inclined to approve. "Are you a friend of Mary's?"

"It is rather difficult to explain who I am and why I am here," Duff said. "Did you know Miss Brown?"

"Miss Brown? Oh, Mary's guest, of course. I was to

meet her this evening. Has she gone? She is a very old friend of Norry's, you know. I mean to say, Dr. Christenson's. He and I— Perhaps you don't know that he is my fiance?"

"I have been told, and I congratulate him," said Duff gallantly. "You never have met Miss Brown, then?"

"No." She frowned politely.

"Miss Brown became ill very suddenly," Duff said, "and has died."

Her cigarette paused in midair at exactly the proper angle of surprise.

Alfie said, "She was poisoned."

An expression of pain crossed Miss Avery's face. Pain or aversion? Distaste was closer.

Duff said, "The doctor was very anxious to spare you the shock of this news. I'm sorry."

She said, "How dreadful!"

"*He's* a detective," announced Alfie, wagging his thumb. "*He's* MacDougal Duff. Mac Duff, you know. He's famous."

Now she looked, in some subtle way, outraged. She crushed out her cigarette. "Really?" she said.

Duff knew he had lost caste, and it amused him.

"Did Dr. Christenson say I was to wait here for him?" she asked.

"He didn't say. I'm sure he plans to be here as soon as he can. I should think you ought to do whatever you like."

She glanced at her watch.

Duff said, "It's too bad this henhouse you speak of has no telephone."

"I have a farm," she said coldly. "I breed dogs,

normally. I have been raising chickens since the war."

Duff made no comment, and Alfie leaped into the breach. "Oh, gosh, you oughta see it. It's right here in New Rochelle, out on the Neck. She's got real barns and cows and everything. She's rich," he added.

Paul knocked an elbow into his ribs. Dinny came downstairs.

Miss Avery seemed mildly pleased with Dinny's admiring hospitality. She thawed out a little and even spoke graciously to Duff from time to time, while Dinny led a bright chat about Miss Avery's dogs and how adorable the puppies were. The boys drifted toward the hall. Soon they had oozed themselves out and away, upstairs.

Duff gleaned what he could. Miss Avery was disposed to be friendly toward Mary, in her condescending way. In her eyes, for some reason, Mary had caste. She was not fond of children but would allow them to admire her if they wished to do so. She was quite absorbed in her own interests and gave an effect of being well pleased with Miss Constance Avery and her ways. To Duff, she seemed essentially chilly and chilling.

At about ten-thirty the doctor came. He brought with him Eve Meredith, the red-headed woman Duff had already seen at the hospital.

The doctor made a bee-line for his fiancee. "My dear, I've called you and called you. I did try to head you off—"

"Yes, I know," she said. "So Mr. Duff said." She smiled graciously, but their greeting included no caress.

"Where were you, darling?"

"Repairing the henhouse," she told him. Duff realized, now, that she spoke as an executive, as a superintendent. Somebody had been repairing the henhouse under her direction.

"Did they tell you?" Eve Meredith was what is known as a bundle of nerves, tied together with a twitching skin. "Oh, Constance, isn't it awful! Dinny, darling, how are you? It must have been just terrible for you. Just terrible. You poor child!"

She clung to Dinny a moment. Dinny looked stoical about it. Duff thought to himself that he understood why this one of Mary's friends had not been asked to stay with the children. Her auburn eyes scurried from face to face. She sat down and held herself together with her arms.

Duff blended himself into the upholstery in a way he had and prepared to listen, taking notes. Dr. Christenson, one saw, was humble before his love. He looked at her constantly. He spoke to her as if he were sweeping the dust before her feet with the plumes on his hat. Miss Avery preened herself, somewhat, in the warmth of this devotion. He had received the accolade. But not Eve. Eve had no caste. Eve was being kindly tolerated, and Eve didn't resent it. Eve was too nervous and strung up to notice much.

It was not long before their stock of exclamations, their little civilized cries of horror and concern, died away. Duff, in his chair, loomed in their consciousness. They turned to him and seemed to wait.

"How is Taffy?" Duff inquired.

"Much better. Much better. She'll be all right."

"Aw, the darling," Dinny murmured, and Duff smiled at her.

"Have you—er—?" The doctor didn't finish the question, as usual. He had a way of opening his eyes very wide behind his glasses and looking earnestly at him whom he questioned, a mannerism that substituted for words.

"Oh, yes, we've been talking," said Duff amiably. "I wish you would tell me what you know about Miss Brown."

"I expect I know all about her," the doctor said, as if this surprised him. "She was an old friend of Mary's and mine, too. That is, I've known her ever since she first began to come to see Mary. Brownie was all right. Good sport, you know. She never married. Had a private income, was able to do pretty much what she liked. Not that she did much, traveled around, visited. She was a good soul."

"She held the mortgage here?"

The doctor looked startled. "Yes, yes, she did. Just to be kind. That was the sort of thing she would do. Never pressed Mary, if Mary had any difficulty. Friendly arrangement, really. Although, of course, it was perfectly businesslike, too."

Dinny looked a little skeptical. When she saw Duff had noticed and was waiting for her comment, she said, "Well, she wasn't so darned businesslike. Sometimes she'd tell Mother there was no hurry or don't bother and just wouldn't take the money, and then again she'd say she expected it right away. Mother wished she'd *be* businesslike."

"Maybe she was a little bit female," the doctor said with half a laugh. "But a good soul. As a matter of fact, she loaned me money, too, long ago. When I was setting myself up in a new set of offices and needed it."

"Did she really?" said Constance remotely.

"Oh, yes. Yes, she did. Poor soul. It was good of her. Furthermore, I've paid interest on it ever since, but never the principal. I suppose I owe it to her estate."

"Who are her heirs?" Duff asked.

"I don't believe I know. She has no relatives left, that I ever heard of."

"She had a snapshot of you as a baby?" Duff said delicately.

The doctor squirmed. "Oh, Lord, yes, of course she did. She swiped it out of a boxful of old stuff I had. That was the sort of thing, the sort of joke, that appealed to Brownie. Do you know what I mean?"

"A lumbering sort of joke," murmured Duff, and the doctor looked satisfied.

Eve Meredith had not uttered a word, but every hair on her head looked furious. Duff turned to her.

"Mrs. Meredith, you knew Miss Brown, too, did you not?"

"Of course I did," she snapped. "I didn't like her." One felt that, because she was so nervous, Eve was bound to be indiscreet and blurt things out. Every so often she would make a remark that seemed like an explosion, forcing its way through a too rigid control that failed to control at all. She exploded now. "As a matter of fact, I never set foot in Mary's house while Brownie was here."

"Why not?" said Duff.

"Because I didn't like her," Eve repeated stubbornly. "She and Mary and I all went to the same school, years ago. Years ago."

Duff asked what school, and she told him, rubbing her neck with one hand as if something had been choking her. "It's eleven o'clock," she said. "I'm going to turn on the news . . . just low."

"Oh, Eve, not now," the doctor begged. "There won't be any."

"I've got to know," said Eve. "No, don't let me bother you. I'll turn it low. But I've got to listen."

She moved jerkily to the far corner where Mary's little table radio stood. She bent over it, and in a moment the familiar cadences of the newscaster came softly forth.

The doctor said to Duff, "Eve's boy is a Marine. She thinks there's going to be another landing any day now."

"She's much too anxious," said Constance righteously. Constance was smoking one cigarette after another in a ladylike disdain, sitting very straight for one who sat on a soft sofa. The doctor sprawled next to her. He looked helpless and tired.

Duff said to him, "I wish you would tell me what you know about the goings-on in this house today. When were you here?"

"Mary called me about . . . oh, three-thirty or four o'clock. Told me Taffy was upset. I was busy as the dickens. For some reason, people seem to feel sicker on the Sabbath. Well, I told her what to do, make Taffy as comfortable as possible. Said I'd get here as quick as I could. Got here, finally, about six. Looked like rain, then, I remember. Went up and had a look at her."

"Who let you in?"

"Nobody. I walked in. I make pretty free of this house, you know. Dinny heard me and shouted, 'Hello.' Well, Mary and I talked about Taffy—"

"Where was Miss Brown?"

"She was on the terrace, then," put in Dinny, "but she must have heard his car or me yelling, because she went upstairs."

"Yes, she did. That's right," said the doctor. "I went across to Mary's desk to write a prescription. Brownie came in, said a few words—"

"What words? Do you remember?"

"Oh, greetings." The doctor put a cigarette in his holder. "I hadn't seen her for about six months, you see. Spoke to her on the phone, yesterday, welcome and all that. Made a date for tonight. I was anxious for her to meet Constance." Constance let him have a chilly smile.

"Anyhow," continued the doctor, "she asked about Taffy—what was the matter . . ."

"What was the matter?"

The doctor shrugged. "I don't know yet," he said smoothly. "We often don't ever know, with these little ones. Let me see. Then Mary came in and told Brownie she'd better go ahead with supper. Brownie went away."

"Downstairs?"

"I really don't know. I imagine so."

"But you saw her again?"

"Oh, yes, certainly. I came down myself in a minute or two. It occurred to me, then, that with Taffy upset it might be better to call off the evening we had planned, so I tried to call Constance."

"When was that, Norry?" Constance asked him.

"Little before six-thirty, or a little after."

"I was very late," she sighed. "You know how I am when I'm interested."

"Then?"

"Brownie had heard me and came out of the dining room—"

"With a wine glass in her hand?"

"Yes, yes . . ."

"And offered you some?"

"Oh, you know that? Yes, she did. She always claimed it was a great tonic, you know, and I rather—er—kidded her about that. It was a little joke. Oh, I sipped it."

"It tasted . . . ?"

"All right." He shrugged again.

"Then?"

"Oh, Dinny went up with a tray . . . let me see . . . Mary called down, something about the food . . ."

"Would Brownie like some bacon," prompted Dinny.

"Yes. Yes, that was it. Well, then I left. Said goodby, see you later, and so forth." The doctor waved his hand. "I had got as far as the front door—"

"Yes, I know," murmured Duff. "You then brought her into this room, and shortly thereafter she died."

"Yes."

Constance's nostrils dilated. She held her head a little higher as if she defied the late presence of death.

"Then?"

"Well, I realized . . . something was wrong. Knew I'd have to call in the coroner. I told everybody to stay away from the food—"

"Did you turn off the toaster?"

"What?"

"The toaster that was set up on the dining room table?"

"Oh. No. No, I did not. Didn't go in there at all. In

74

fact, I was immediately busy arranging to get Taffy to the hospital. I called there. I also called the police and reported what had happened. I went out to my car."

"Before it began to rain so hard."

"Yes. Yes, of course. Then it did rain hard, and I had to stay where I was."

"The next," sighed Duff, "I know. The police arrived, I suppose, soon after we had gone?"

"Oh, almost immediately. Let's see. Dinny, you were on the stairs when I got back in. And Paul had come indoors, I think. I was talking to them when the police car drove into the drive."

"I wonder," said Duff, "who turned off that toaster."

"It is off, then?"

"Oh, yes. We could see through the glass."

"I wonder how any of it happened," said the doctor in sudden depression. "A thing like that. Terrible."

"Dreadful," said Constance.

"Why did you send Taffy to the hospital?" said Duff, so abruptly that it had a brutal sound.

"Why . . . why, she was quite s-sick . . ." the doctor stuttered.

"Couldn't she have been sick in her own bed?" inquired Duff silkily. "Really? It doesn't seem to be serious. It seems to me that Mrs. Moriarity was put in a very uncomfortable position, having to leave her children here with things as they are."

"I was thinking of my patient," said the doctor with great dignity. "Believe me, little Taffy is better off where she is."

Eve made a convulsive movement in her corner. The radio was quiet now. She was watching with her strained reddish eyes.

"Oh, yes," she twittered in unexpected support, "much better. Much better." She began to twist a ring around and around her finger.

Duff smelled a rat. He said nothing about it, but a shiver crept along his nerves again.

"You have no news yet about what the poison actually was?" he inquired of the doctor.

"No, sir. Not yet."

"Or where it was," mused Duff. "The evidence that it was in the wine seems confused."

"I think it was in the wine."

"In which bottle?"

"Which bottle! Were there two?"

"Oh, yes. Two bottles of Dubonnet. Just alike. No one knows where the second bottle came from, unless Mrs. Moriarity can say."

"A bottle of Dubonnet?" said Eve shrilly. "I gave her a bottle of Dubonnet this afternoon." She came toward them, looking desperate.

"You were here, Mrs. Meredith?"

"No. Brownie came to my house." The thin woman had thrown her head back, and the cords in her neck were ugly to see.

"Won't you please sit down and tell me about it?"

She sat down on the very edge of a chair and turned to him her haggard face. "I never came here while she was here, and she never came to see me. But today was different. Mary had to have my ice collar for Taffy. The children weren't around, or at least, only the baby. Mary asked me for it over the phone. She was welcome, of course. But I had been lying down. I wasn't dressed. So"—the woman shrugged, and Duff thought her bones would rattle—"she sent Brownie, and Brownie came over. Oh, she came stomping over through the gate."

"Did you talk with her at all?"

"Hardly at all. Hardly at all. I called down that I was hunting for it. She stayed in my living room. When I brought it down I felt . . . oh . . . well . . . After all, she was in my house. I felt . . ."

"Conciliatory?" suggested Duff.

"Yes," said Eve. "Yes, I guess so. I do things impulsively sometimes. I gave her that bottle of wine. I knew she liked it. Gimme a light, Norry."

The cigarette bobbed in her lips. She took it out and blew a long streamer of smoke. "Well?" she said. "It wasn't poisoned."

"How are you sure, Mrs. Meredith?"

"Because I had some of it myself," she said hoarsely. "Somebody gave it to me, you know. I didn't buy it. Well, I tried some." She made a face.

"It had been opened, then, when you gave it to her?"

"Yes, that's what I'm saying. I opened it last week."

"I see."

"And it was perfectly all right. I'll swear to that." She repeated, "I'll swear to that."

"Good heavens, Mrs. Meredith, you wouldn't have given it to her otherwise," said Constance Avery primly.

Eve quivered and stood up. "That's all I know," she said. "I went on duty at the hospital at five-thirty. I'm tired. I've got to get some rest." She looked around and shuddered. "Well, good night. No, don't come, Norry. It's just next door, after all. Dinny, darling, if there's anything I can do . . ."

Dinny said, gently, her voice suddenly modulated,

77

tactful, grownup, "Oh, Aunt Eve, I don't think so. We're fine. I'd come over and stay with *you*, but I don't think I'd better leave Davey when Mother isn't here."

"No, dear. No, of course not. You're a sweet thing."

"Try to sleep," said Dinny in a motherly fashion. "Just relax, Aunt Eve. Please do." She seemed very strong and cool and wise, helping the older woman to the door. It was a part. There was something in this odd-looking girl that transcended her appearance. She would be, Duff thought in his prophetic soul, an actress, after all.

Then Duff remembered something. "I have a message for you, Doctor. Somebody who said he was Oliver O'Leary . . ."

"Yes?"

"Called and wants you to call him as soon as you can." The doctor did not hurry to the phone. "I hope you know where to find him," said Duff.

"Oh, yes, of course. Patient of mine. As a matter of fact, he is staying at my house."

"Oh?" Duff waited, looking as if he didn't believe a word of it. But no one said anything. Dinny came back from the hall.

"Is there any reason," said Duff bluntly, "why Mr. O'Leary calls a man, answering the phone from this house, Professor Moriarity?"

"Uh? Professor? Good heavens, I don't know. O'Leary is a strange fellow. Nervous about himself, you know. Odd. Very odd. Likes to keep in touch. Er . . . I'll ask him. Shall I?"

Duff, watching Dinny's plump hands with the childish ring on one of them, saw that they remained quiet and relaxed. She seemed very politely interested.

This was her role, of course.

"It's getting late," said Constance.

"Dinny, my child, you go to bed," said the doctor.

"I want to show Mr. Duff where he's going to sleep," she said quietly. "Would you mind being in my room, sir? I think I'd better climb in with the little ones. I assure you, I'd do that anyway."

"All right," said Duff, amused, though he couldn't help being touched, too. She thought he wouldn't care for Brownie's place. "And I know where that is. Thank you, Dinny."

She said good night in character, in this serene, responsible manner she'd assumed for Eve. Then she let a touch of the child sneak back. "I don't suppose we're allowed to get breakfast," she said wistfully.

"We'll send out for hamburgers," Duff told her, and she laughed very gaily, with a soupçon of the sophisticate, and made her exit.

"A sweet girl," said Dr. Christenson. "A very sweet child. Mary's children are a fine lot."

"And *such* a lot," said Constance with a little metallic shudder of laughter. "Shall we be going along, Norry?"

"Yes, I think so." The doctor looked nervously at Duff. "I do hope . . . I should think . . ." he blundered. "I was wondering . . . if you wouldn't find some evidence that poison had been brought into the house by mistake. Something of that sort? With the children, and all, and the house a little upset. A terrible thing, you know, but . . ." He stuck.

"Accidental," Duff finished for him.

"After all, it must have been. It couldn't have been anything else."

79

Miss Avery was putting on her gloves and saying nothing.

Duff looked the doctor in the eye. "What are you afraid of?"

"I?"

"Yes. What is it? What's bothering you?"

"Mary didn't . . . ?" The doctor appealed.

"Mary didn't tell me, if that's what you mean to ask."

"Then ask Mary," the doctor said. "I can't . . . really . . ."

"Come," said Duff, "if I do ask Mary, you expect her to tell me?"

"Yes. Yes, I . . . But I don't like to. Look, Mr. Duff, I think you're with us on this. Ask Mary about a certain conversation at the breakfast table."

"This morning?"

"Yes."

"With Brownie?"

"No, no. She wasn't up."

"*About* Brownie?"

"Yes. Please ask Mary."

"Mary," said Duff slowly, "hinted, did she not, that for some reason Brownie was becoming somewhat of a nuisance?"

"She did tell you!" The doctor looked startled again.

"Perhaps."

The doctor licked his lips. "Well?"

"And yet she didn't," Duff said. "Will you tell me this much? To whom did Mary drop this . . . hint? Whatever it was?" The doctor stood dumbly. "Who was there at the breakfast table this morning?" Duff insisted.

"Just the children," Dr. Christenson said.

"Yes," said Duff heavily, "yes, as you say, of course. The children. All of them?"

"I believe they were all there," the doctor said sadly. "Terrible thing. I do hope . . . Well . . . Ready, darling?"

Constance Avery bowed, from the neck. She held no white glove out to Duff, the detective. "Good night," she said brightly, as to a doorman.

CHAPTER 6

Duff went around closing windows and locking them, testing doors. He did not know whether this was the Moriarity custom, but the window screens were only half-screens with handles inside by which they could be pushed up. Duff felt that the absence of handles on the outside would not prevent a determined person from raising them. So he locked the windows, wishing to err on the side of caution. Gathering up his bag, which he had left in the hall on his first entrance, he went up the creaking stairs to Dinny's room.

The big old house was quiet, except for the kind of breathing an old house does at night. It did not feel empty. The presence of sleeping children was somehow evident. There was nothing weird or sinister in the near-silence. It was simply an old, shabby, well-inhabited house on a quiet street.

Duff prepared for bed and turned out his light. He stood in Dinny's window, looking out at the dim garden. No moon tonight, but a street light filtered through the trees.

These kids. Duff sorted them in his mind, let his impressions flow together, tried, as he so often had, to lean on his intuition. It seemed to him that they were conspirators. He liked them—oh, very much. They were delightful. Nevertheless, they were allied to keep something out of his knowledge.

Mary was worried about the kids.

Duff began to face it. Mary was afraid that the kids might have, in some childish, half-innocent way, caused Brownie's death. There it was. That was the thing that frightened Mary, and frightened Duff, too.

However, and of this he felt certain, they were not conspirators in Brownie's death. These children were not allied to commit murder and conceal their crime. An impossible idea! Not tenable.

Yet, he supposed, one conspirator could have a deeper secret of his own. But . . .

Duff yanked his mind again and forced it to the thing that must be faced, the most frightening thought of all. One little person was not a conspirator, and that was the one they had rushed away, put away safe, for given reasons that were not too adequate. One little person, just old enough to understand what poison is, and young enough to be still unmoral, as a baby is. . . . Who had been playing nurse, giving medicine to her dolls. . . . Who had suffered injustice from Miss Emily Brown. . . . Who, even though she may have long forgotten the incident, may have kept a feeling of being out of sympathy. . . . Duff's heart shouted No! But his mind went on. A little person who had heard her mother say . . . and to her, Mother must seem infallible, like God.

And, worst, a little person about whom Eve knew a secret. Eve had been at the hospital. *Why* was Taffy better off in the hospital? *Why* must she be out of the house before the police came? If Eve knew, did Mary know, too? Did the doctor know?

Yes, he thought the doctor knew.

Oh, Taffy wouldn't count as a murderer. She would count as an accident. God help her. Duff felt sick. For the first time, since he had won the battle of self-integration, long ago, he found that he was unwilling to follow passively wherever the truth led. *If* it should lead this way. No! Not Taffy! *No!* He knew his mind to be scrambling for some sand under which to rest its metaphorical head, and he let it go. If this were so, he didn't want to know it. If it looked as if it were going to be so, he would hang onto doubt, keep doubt handy, to hide in, to give her the benefit of . . . for the rest of her life.

But there was plenty of doubt, after all. There was, for instance, Eve herself. He must ferret out what the feud was about and how seriously those two women were enemies. Eve, the nervous wreck, might . . . might, mind you . . . think she could get away with so simple a device as handing the woman a bottle of poisoned wine. There was a possible motive, a possible method, both sounding very obvious and too simple. Still, they must be checked. A simple, obvious, half-crazy way of killing. Maybe.

Who else? Where could he find more doubt? Another suspect. The man who was hidden in the house. Professor Moriarity?

Come, thought Duff, why should a man hide in a house anyway? Would he hide for the purpose of getting at Brownie? Then the motive must be important and urgent. What motive? None known.

Or was he hiding for some other reason and had he been discovered by Brownie, and therefore, to maintain his concealment. . . . ? Brownie may have gone quietly or suddenly into her room, that room through which the back stairs passed, and seen what she shouldn't have seen. Found out what she mustn't know, or at least mustn't tell.

Now, why does a man hide? What makes it as important as that to stay hidden? When he is afraid for his life. For his fortune. When he is running from the law.

Haggerty and his escaped convict! Duff thought that an escaped convict hiding in the house would come in very handy. Except for the fact that only one man, convict or not, could possibly command the cooperation of the Moriarity kids. Duff sighed. Still a family affair.

Could a man hide here without the kids knowing?

Duff thought not.

However, let us see. There was that clipping, the one Brownie had treasured, about the actor and the runaway woman and the auto accident. Professor Moriarity? They said he was an actor. Who, then, would the woman be? And even so, unless this could somehow be twisted to mean that missing urgent motive, what bearing could it have?

Duff smiled to himself. He had nothing against a coincidence. They are elements of reality, after all. The only coincidence was the word "actor." Lots of men were actors. His real conviction was that the clipping meant the gray hair ad. Awkwardly cut out, so as to save the address. The clipping was quite fresh, consistent with Brownie's growing older. It was not, for instance, a record or reminder of some old trouble about which she had been blackmailing.

For she might have been a blackmailer, in a hearty good-scoutish kind of way. His picture of Brownie admitted that. A woman who liked to crack little whips, liked enough power over her friends to make her whims important. A good soul, kindhearted and petty, jolly, and just a little cruel, for fun.

Dr. Christenson said he'd been paying interest on a loan. But was there ever a loan? Or were the payments something else? Although Dr. Christenson was no actor.

Haggerty. O'Leary. Moriarity. Very Hibernian flavor to Duff's world, suddenly. The Irish are proud of being Irish, aren't they? He wished he had a picture of Mary's husband.

Yes, he must have that, must find one. He awoke to his surroundings, switched on Dinny's lamp again, and looked carefully at the snapshots stuck into her mirror, at the few other photographs in the room. Lots and lots of girls, some boys, several dogs, one cat, no fathers.

Duff turned the light off and got into Dinny's rather hard little bed. He was too long for it. He was always too long. A pattern of leaves moved on the ceiling in

86

silhouette. Country quiet out here. Would there be a cock crow? Chickens. Constance Avery.

Ah ha, there's a one! Duff thought to himself: My fine lady, wouldn't I just like to pin this rap on you! Right on your rosy fingernails. A henhouse alibi. Had he better check? No, not so. When it's poison, alibis are not convincing. Poison can go into a bottle and sit and wait until the victim gets around to taking it. That is, it can, if anyone can ever figure out the tangled evidence about those wine bottles.

Hm. Brownie sipped wine on the terrace. And lived. No good. We don't know which bottle. Or do we? The bought bottle, of course, for Eve's was open already. Therefore, since both bottles had been opened by the time Dinny came home, Brownie had opened her own. Duff didn't know what difference it made.

He thought of Alfie, on the back porch in the rain. Alfie couldn't have done anything then, although he was there alone, outside the empty dining room. But too late. Too late. Besides . . . not Alfie. *Not Taffy!*

Duff embarked, for comfort, on a fantasy. Suppose Brownie and the doctor to have had a love affair, long ago. Of course, the baby. Maybe the baby had been rung in on Mary's family. No, too old. None of these kids, he was willing to bet, had ever worn embroidered petticoats. Ah, well . . . say Constance discovers all. Mad with jealousy, she . . . Hm.

There was a sound in the old house too regular to be the normal creaking of its timber bones. A measured pace. *Thump, thump, thump, thump . . . wheeeeee, thump.* It was what music did in the movies, in a funny movie when there was going to be a ghost.

Duff heaved himself out of bed, then listened again. No, he was wrong. It was not that insulting rhythm, after all. But it was footsteps.

"Damn it," said MacDougal Duff, wrapping his robe around him. "there *is* a bogey man!"

He got very quietly to the top of the stairs, on the third floor. Puzzling swishes and soft bumps seemed to surround him. He had his flash, but he did not turn it on until he had softly opened the door to the boys' room. The boys were two silent humps. But were the humps boys? Duff crossed over and investigated. They were boys, all right. Sweetly and innocently asleep, breathing gently.

Duff's light wavered away across the wall, and Alfie stirred and sat up. "What's the matter?"

"Never mind." Duff would have fled, but Alfie was pounding Paul, and the two of them made a hushed uproar of alarm and question.

So he posted one of them at the top of each stairs and searched, finding nothing.

The whole time he had an absurd vision of Mr. Moriarity tiptoeing about just ahead of him, and once he even turned suddenly in his tracks to catch him if he were behind.

Nothing.

Duff went grimly down to the second floor. In the big bedroom Dinny was curled protectively around her baby brother, both sleeping sweetly and innocently. In the other bed Mitch heaved her curly top up and said, "What's the matter?"

"*Ssh*," said Duff mysteriously. "I'm the night watchman."

She lay back and seemed to accept these goings-on

as just one more incomprehensible adult activity, one more queer grownup habit she hadn't encountered before, to be sure, but which would never be fully explained until she was grown up herself.

Feeling very foolish, Duff went downstairs. The boys hung over the stairwell, high up. He paid no attention to them. He began the rounds conscientiously, testing all entries. The cellar door, which had been locked, was not locked any more. There was a key on the inside. He had noticed a key on the outside. The key that had been on the outside, or at least a key, lay on the floor.

Duff slipped his light around the cellar. Nothing. It was a big open space, no partitions. A ping-pong table stood hard by the furnace. Nothing. Nobody.

Duff came back up and stood frowning at the key when there was a faint tap on the outside door, the one dubbed the back door, although it led to the driveway on the side.

"Who's that?" Was the bogey man locked out?

Duff opened cautiously to the solemn and somehow conspiratorial face of Mr. Haggerty. "Good evening," said that one. "I happened to see your light."

"That was quite a happening," said Duff tartly, "since to see it you must have been lurking in the driveway."

"It so happens I was," said Mr. Haggerty. He lifted his brows. His melancholy eyes popped a little. "Any—er—trouble?"

MacDougal Duff began to laugh. The ridiculous delicacy this fellow put into his impertinence reminded him of Charlie Chaplin in the old days. That same fussy, formal, exaggerated, self-confident absurdity as when Charlie used to flit over the screen, dusting with gay abandon, after having been caught doing something he shouldn't. And Duff himself was cast in the role of the suspicious, glaring, menacing authority who had caught him and under whose eye the pitiful and hilarious attempt to deceive took place.

"No, no trouble," Duff said at last. "A little haunting, perhaps. These old houses . . ."

"I happen to know," said Haggerty, "that there was someone in your cellar a minute ago."

"Indeed?"

"Oh, yes. I heard someone. No lights were shown. But someone came up from there and, I believe, opened this door."

"It's possible," Duff said. "What were you doing out here?"

"Keeping an eye out," Haggerty said. "I warned you I wouldn't give up, you know."

"Did you happen to see a light in the attic, longer ago than ten minutes?"

"That I can't see from here." Haggerty looked extremely apologetic within his curious dignity.

"Mr. Haggerty, I don't suppose I can persuade you not to hang around any longer?"

"Oh, no. I've had a very interesting time, so far."

Duff leaned back against the wall. "Who was in the cellar?"

"Who? I can't say."

"Was it you?"

"Me?" He answered a question with a question. "How would I get in?"

Duff said, "I'm going to bed. Good night."

"Wait. I . . . er"—the fellow cleared his throat —"saw Miss Brown's will."

"You mean, of course, that you *happened* to see it," said Duff after a moment. "All right. What was in it?"

"She tears up the mortgage," said Haggerty with a fine dramatic gesture. "Also . . . also"—he held the tidbit tantalizingly—"she forgives Dr. Christenson his debts. She forgives everybody."

"Who is everybody?"

"People in California." Haggerty intoned his next like the end of *Hamlet*. "The rest," he said, "is charity."

Duff shook his head. "She had loaned the doctor money?"

"Yes, indeed," said Haggerty promptly. "Five thousand dollars. Fifteen years ago."

"A genuine loan?"

Haggerty pricked up his ears. "What's that?"

"Just the death rattle of a little notion," Duff said. "I do thank you."

"Oh, thank *you*," said Haggerty. "I'll call again."

Duff closed and locked the back door and went upstairs, thinking. Now, if, when Haggerty was here earlier, he had nipped around and got in at the back, he *might* have flushed that toilet. Might have had time, that is. Although how he could have made such a betraying error . . . Reflex, he thought.

The boys were still hanging over the rail. "Who was that?" they demanded.

"Our friend, Mr. Haggerty," Duff told them. "Go back to bed. I'm baffled." They hesitated. "If that's any comfort to you," Duff added, a trifle nastily.

They vanished then. Duff stood in the second-floor

hall and sniffed the air. Someone had been smoking here. He smelled tobacco. Now, Haggerty had not been smoking on the second floor while talking to Duff in the back hall. Not he.

"What I need," said Duff to himself grimly, "is my little monograph on the varieties of tobacco ash. Or the needle, Watson."

CHAPTER 7

Dawn came up over the high evergreen hedges at the edge of Mary's garden and blazed in full bright at the eastern window of Dinny's room. It was too bright for Duff, and he woke. He was standing at the back window, looking out over the narrow porch roof to see how the stable lay, there at the end of the drive, in the corner of the property, and how low hedges fenced off the vegetables beyond the back lawn, and how a curving back lane bounded the place in that direction, when there came a tap at his door.

It was Dinny herself in a blue calico skirt and a thin white blouse. "Hello. I thought maybe you'd want to know that those men are back. The ones who were here? They say it's all right to get breakfast. So shall I?"

"It sounds like a good idea," he said, smiling. "Did you sleep well?"

"Of course," she said wonderingly. "Did you?"

"As a matter of fact, I did. It's very quiet here."

"We like it," Dinny said. "Of course, we've always

93

lived here. I guess we wouldn't know how to act anywhere else. I'll make you some coffee."

Duff sniffed. "Don't you mean you already have?"

"I took a chance," said Dinny swiftly and went away.

Duff turned thoughtfully back into the room and walked again to the south window. He was organizing his problems. His eyes, unfocused, were caught by a difference in the view, and slowly he brought his gaze in toward what was different. On the red porch roof that had been bare a moment ago, there now lay a neat pair of eggshells. And not birds' eggs, either. Hen's eggs. Breakfast eggs.

Duff looked at them for a long minute. Then he put on his coat and went downstairs.

Pring said, "Good morning." The two detectives looked very dewy with their clean shirts and their fresh shaves. They appeared to be waiting for him in the hall. "How'd it go?"

"Why," said Duff, "once I thought I heard something, and I got up and looked, but there was no one there. News?"

"Yep," Pring said. "We got the poison. It was in the wine, all right."

"It really was, eh?"

"Yep. Nicotine."

"Nicotine."

"Yep. In the dregs of her glass. In the bottle that was on the table. In the body. No place else."

"That seems to have been enough," Duff said.

"Yeah, it was plenty. Well, the next thing . . . we got fingerprints off them bottles. And that's a funny thing."

"Tell me."

"Well, on the bottle that had the poison, the one we found on the table, there was the dead woman's prints and the girl's, the oldest girl."

"Dinny?"

"Yeah, and a set we don't have. Female, or seems like it."

"Yes?"

"Not Mrs. Moriarity," said Robin. "Not if she brushes her own hair."

"We took her hairbrush," explained Pring to Duff's narrowed eyes.

"Yes, of course. But—that's all?"

"That's all. On that bottle. But what I mean is funny . . . on the bottle that we found in the pantry, the one that isn't poisoned at all, perfectly good wine . . . on *that* bottle there aren't *any* fingerprints."

"That's odd."

"You're telling me! I don't make head nor tail of those wine bottles. I was trying to figure it out, see. Now, the bottle on the table . . . she pours herself a glass, takes it out in the hall, gives the doc a swig, so it's O.K. So I figured, first, it must be somebody switched bottles there. While she was out in the hall. But the girl says she gave her mother a drink out of the other bottle. So *it* wasn't poisoned either. Not at that time. Finally, I see a light. That first glass she poured herself musta come out of the pantry, the good bottle. Trouble is, now we got the girl's fingerprints on the wrong bottle, unless she touched them both."

"You didn't hear about the little fellow," Duff said pityingly. And told him about Davey.

"Yeah? So where's *his* prints?" Pring demanded.

"Somebody wiped them off the bottle you found in the pantry."

"But it musta been on the table when he took some."

"The bottles were switched."

"Yeah, but when?"

"It's a cinch they got switched before she took that poisoned swallow," Robin said.

"O.K." said Pring. "So it's in between when the little kid took some and when she came back to the table."

"Therefore," said Duff, "very likely it was young Mitch who switched them. Still . . ."

"Why?" said Pring suspiciously. "Why would she?"

"Why? Perhaps the boy spilled it in pouring, messed up the neck of the bottle. Something of the sort. She might, therefore, wipe it off, you see?"

"Sure. Sure," said Robin in excitement. "Wipe it off, and then change bottles because more was gone than oughta be. Hm? Whadda ya say?"

"So Bottle B, from the pantry, gets to the table and Brownie dies of it. But," Duff reminded them, "after all, Mrs. Moriarity does not die."

"We better ask her . . ." Pring stopped and chewed his lip.

"Maybe she didn't drink it," Robin blurted.

"That's what I have been wondering," Duff told him.

"Yeah? Why wouldn't she?" Pring's eyes looked hard and suspicious again.

"Dinny put it on her tray to be thoughtful. But if Mrs. Moriarity didn't care for it . . ."

"I gotcha," Robin said. "It was kinda cute of the kid.

Her mother wouldn't want to hurt her feelings. I think you got it, Mr. Duff."

"I think he's working for Mrs. Moriarity," said Pring dryly.

"It doesn't matter who I'm working for," said Duff with a hidden twinge. "Let me ask you, have you looked for a napkin or rag or towel stained with wine that Mitch might have used to wipe the bottle?" They didn't answer. "And then again," Duff went on gently, "you did take her fingerprints, did you not? Why are the third prints you find on the poisoned bottle strange to you? How did Mitch carry it? In her teeth? And if with gloves or their equivalent, why?"

"So when she wiped off the bottle, it was *after* she moved it," Pring snapped and turned to Robin. "Go root around for that rag. And find that kid."

"After she moved which bottle?" Duff insisted softly. "She didn't wipe both, you know. Although she moved both, if any."

Pring gave him a disgusted look and strode to the telephone. "I'm going to find out when we can get ahold of Mrs. Moriarity."

Duff said, "I'll use the phone after you," and strolled through the now open glass door into the dining room.

It was a pleasant sunny room, here on the east and south, facing the garden both ways. There was a crusted place on the rug, an ugly and tragic mess. Poor woman. Duff turned away from it. The oval dining-room table was drawn toward the back windows, the long windows that led to the porch. Duff studied it, noted the toaster still plugged into the wall socket.

Dinny put her head in through the swinging pantry

door. "Breakfast's in the kitchen. The cleaners are coming . . ."

"Come in here a minute. Tell me who sat where."

She approached the table, skirting the bad place on the floor with delicate courage. "I was up here in Mother's place." She indicated the end of the table toward the front hall, where, if one sat, one would have one's back turned to the rest of the house. "Paul was supposed to be here, on my left. But he hadn't come in. Then Brownie. Taffy's regular place." This faced the pantry, Duff noted, and one sitting there would be well able to see the doctor as he came downstairs. "Then Davey. Then Mitch." The two littlest were spaced around the far end. "Then Alfie, and then nobody, because that's where I usually sit."

"Thank you," Duff said. He ran his eyes over the crumpled napkins. One lay on the floor. One lay in Mitch's chair, and it was stained with wine. "Is Mr. Robin in the kitchen?"

"Yes, he's poking around all over."

"Tell him to come in here a minute."

Robin came and looked at Mitch's napkin. "So she did wipe it off. Good guess, Mr. Duff."

"Have you found her?"

Robin jerked his head toward the kitchen, and he and Duff went through the little square pantry, so near the back stairs, into the big and much dimmer kitchen, where Dinny had set out breakfast on the linoleum-topped table, and where Mitch and Davey, side by side, were lapping up bowls of cereal like little lambs.

Pring came in by the other door. He took one of the chairs and turned it sideways, sat down. "Your name is

Mitch? That's what they call you?" He creased his face with a smile.

Mitch flicked her long black lashes and pursued rice crispies without comment.

"Look, suppose you tell me, if you can, huh, when your little brother took some wine, you say you didn't want Miss Brown to know it?"

"That's right," said Mitch.

"So what did you do? Try and tell me now."

"I took it away from him and washed out the glass."

"But he'd drunk some, huh?"

"*Umhum.*" Mitch's head went up and down affirmatively.

Davey said, "Bit"—Davey for "but"—"I lo-ove wine."

Dinny, standing behind him, put her hands on his cheeks caressingly. It looked as if she were holding his jaw shut.

"O.K." said Pring, stretching his mouth in another smile. Duff and Robin were watching silently from near the pantry door. Mitch didn't seem bothered by her audience. She seemed quite happy. She turned her spoon daintily in her hand.

"Now, did you wipe the bottle off any? I guess it was kinda sticky, huh?"

"Certainly I wiped it off," Mitch said indignantly as if he had questioned her housekeeping.

"You did, eh? With your napkin?"

Mitch nodded.

"Oh, Mitch," wailed Dinny, "and it stains!"

Mitch kept her eyes steadily on Pring's. "What else would you like to know?" she asked, and lifted her milk and tossed off the last swallow as if it had been a cocktail.

"I would like to know what else you did, huh?"

"What else? I washed the glass and I dried it and I brought it back and I dumped some of my milk in it. So it wouldn't look too clean, of course."

"Naturally," said Duff. He couldn't help it. Mitch looked up at him and winked.

Pring looked stern. "But you thought they might notice some wine was gone, so you changed the bottles around?"

"*Uhuh.*" Her curls flew from side to side. It seemed a perfectly spontaneous negative.

"Why didn't you?" Pring said.

Mitch looked at him solemnly. "Because I didn't think of it."

"Are you sure?"

"Am I sure what?"

"You didn't move the bottles? You didn't take the one on the table and put it in the pantry and take the one in the pantry and put it on the table?"

"I don't think so," said Mitch as if she were considering the idea quite abstractly.

"Did she, Davey?" said Dinny softly.

Davey said, "Yes, she did."

"I did not!"

"You did too!"

"Da-avey! You're a not-so!"

"I am not a not-so. Not today," said Davey.

Mitch looked at the men, a little worried now. "Are you going to put me in jail?" she asked.

At this Davey's ears got red, and he began suddenly to howl.

Pring, escaped from the uproar into the front hall, mopped his face and said, "What did I do wrong, for the love of Pete?"

"You were doing swell," Robin assured him.

"Yeah, but those kids! Listen, would you say she swapped those bottles? Or didn't she?"

"I'd say no," said Robin, cocking his head on his fat neck.

"Then why'd she think she was going to jail, if she wasn't telling a lie?" He swung around to Duff, who was just coming toward them. "What did you make out of that?"

Duff shrugged. "It seems to me that she didn't switch the bottles," he said, "and yet . . ."

He knew, as they did not, that this wasn't Mitch's first denial. That lovely spontaneity was a repetition. And now Davey said she lied.

"You can't believe Davey," he said aloud.

"Yeah. And yet." Pring was gloomy.

"Tough going," said Duff sympathetically. "Did you reach Mrs. Moriarity?"

"She and the other kid are coming home around noon."

"Oh?"

"Yeah, the kid's better. I think I'll wait and come back. See her here. Well, we're going out in the stable a minute, see if we missed anything."

"Any nicotine?"

"We didn't miss that. It was there, all right. Got it last night. Nicotine sulphate, for bugs." Pring sounded disgusted.

Duff raised his brows. "Still there last night?"

"Who knows how many of those little bottles she

had? And the one we found isn't full."

"Fingerprints? Or was it wiped clean, too?"

"Nobody's fingerprints on any of them poisons," Robin said, "except the big boy's. That's Paul."

"Paul. I believe he works in the garden a good deal."

"That so?"

"So they tell me. I wonder if you know . . ." Duff pulled his lip. "Is nicotine a stomach poison or a contact poison?"

"Contact," Robin said promptly. "I got roses."

"Roses," Duff murmured.

Pring leaned on the newel post and considered Duff insolently. "Seems to me," he drawled, "that we haven't heard much about what you been thinking or doing. Is this a one-way business?"

"Not at all," Duff assured them. He made a lightning decision. "Do you know Eve Meredith?"

"Yeah, sure. Lady next door?"

"Do you know she had a feud on with Emily Brown?"

"Yeah?"

"That she never came into this house while Miss Brown was here? That Miss Brown had done something, said something, long ago? I don't know yet just what. Did you know that Miss Brown went over to her house yesterday afternoon to borrow an ice collar for the sick little girl? That Mrs. Meredith had a bottle of Dubonnet she says was given her? She says she herself had opened it. She says she herself had tasted it. Did you know that she gave that bottle to Miss Brown as a present? That it was the second bottle, the mysterious one? Do you know whether Mrs. Meredith has a garden?"

"Has she?"

"I'm asking," said Duff.

"Yeah, she's got a garden, too," said Robin.

Pring looked as if he were about to whistle.

Duff said carefully, "I don't want to throw her to the wolves. I don't mean to. She seems to me not very well, and extremely nervous. I'd be careful, if I were you. She looks as if she might go off into hysterics any minute, and then what would you know?"

"I'll go easy," Pring said. "Thanks a lot."

Their faces were all relaxed. Duff knew this was dangerous. He'd sent them to poke their noses close to some secret he didn't yet know himself. Close to Eve's dangerous semi-hysterical state. But he'd had to give them something. The advantages of their confidence were great. He could not give them the hidden man, Professor Moriarty. The evidence was so flimsy and ridiculous. Eggshells, tobacco smoke, bumps in the night, and a toilet flushing. He hoped Eve Meredith would keep them busy and keep what there was of her head.

He said, "You're very welcome. Tell me a couple of things more, will you? Did you turn off that toaster, the one that's on the table in there, when you got here last night?"

"Hm?"

"Nope."

"You did not?"

"We did not," said Pring.

"It bothers me some," Duff said. "None of the children big or small, and I've just asked the smallest, seem to have done so. We can take it that Miss Brown didn't. The doctor didn't. Mrs. Moriarity, so I hear,

103

wasn't in the dining room at all after it happened. Or before, either. Who turned off the toaster?"

"Maybe it was the photographer, or some of those guys," Robin offered. "I'll find out."

"Nuts," said Pring. "If you ask me, it could have been the small children, either one of 'em, whatever they say. You said yourself you can't trust the little kid. And if you asked him just now, you picked a bum time to ask him."

"Still," Duff said, "Dinny tells me she believes it was still on when she took the little kids out of the room. She says it crossed her mind to do something about it, and then, in the excitement, she didn't. That's support, perhaps."

"Hm. She tell you that last night?"

"No," Duff admitted.

Pring threw out his hands. "Kids!" he said.

"I wish you'd tell me about this escaped convict." Duff's switch of subject shocked them.

"What escaped convict's that? Oh, you mean that fellow Severson?"

"Do I?"

"Fellow the coroner was talking about last night? Yeah, well, seems they were bringing him up to White Plains, and he walked out on them."

"What's his crime?"

"I dunno. Forgery, or something like that. He wasn't any convict. Had to stand trial. He was pretty slick, and everybody's wild. We got orders to comb the woods for him."

"You have his description?"

"Sure." Robin began to quote. A conscientious man, Robin. "Five foot eleven. Weight, a hunnert and sixty.

Brown eyes, black hair, swarthy complexion, mole under right ear . . ."

"Severson, you say? His right name?"

"Olaf Severson. That's what we've got. Say, who can tell his right name? Though he don't sound like a Swede, at that."

"There are black Norwegians," said Duff, "but he doesn't sound—er—right. He doesn't sound like an Irishman, either."

"What's on your mind?"

"Eggshells," said Duff. "Don't mind me. Do you know a newspaperman name of Haggerty?"

"Never heard of him."

"Is that so? Well, perhaps you will. He's been hanging around here."

"We'll deal with the press," Pring said with dignity. "Any time, Mr. Duff, you want to tell us what you mean by eggshells, we'll listen."

"Listen," said Robin, "no escaped prisoner is going to sneak into a strange house and put poison in a bottle of wine! That don't make sense."

"Who said it did?" Pring snapped. Then to Duff, "You coming out to the stable with us?"

Duff said he thought he'd have some breakfast instead. And what was Miss Brown's address in New York?

There were things in the stable he wanted to examine privately.

CHAPTER 8

He used the telephone first. He called Maguire in town.
Maguire was a little man whose short legs had carried
him on Duff's business before. Duff gave him
Brownie's address. "I want you to go up there and find
out what you can about her. Take a look at how she
lived if you can get in. See if you can dig up somebody
who can give her a past. I want to know about some
goings-on with a woman named Eve Norden,
schoolmate of this Brown's." He gave the school. "Eve
Norden is now Mrs. Meredith. Find out why they had a
feud on. You may have to go all the way back to the
school. Don't hesitate to travel. Dig me up enemies,
any others. Also, what's in her safe-deposit box? That's
a tough one. Find her lawyer, if any. When you run
into authority, you're working for me. I'm working for
Mrs. Moriarity. See if you can find out how this Brown
felt about Mr. Moriarity, husband or ex-husband of
another schoolmate."

"O.K." said Maguire cheerfully, as Duff stopped

speaking. One never needed to repeat. He soaked up Duff's words and would retain them. "Anything else?"

"If you have a spare moment, look up an ex-newspaperman who calls himself Haggerty. I want to know if he exists. Also, look up one Olaf Severson, mixed up with the law out here at the moment. How far back does his background go? In other words, how long has he existed. That's all." He gave his own whereabouts.

As he hung up, he reflected that he had not asked for the most obvious kind of check. He had not asked Maguire to trot around to theatrical agencies and find out where an actor named Moriarity had got to now.

But if at any time he needed to know, he could, of course, ask Mary.

Duff shook himself and proceeded to the kitchen, where Dinny was washing up after the kids. The boys, she said, were not down yet. Davey and Mitch had gone out to play.

"Would you like an egg or anything?"

Duff said he thought not. She brought his coffee and slid into a chair beside him, elbows on the table, round chin in her hands. Very innocent she looked, as if she were sitting at the feet of his superior wisdom. Duff wondered. "Diana Moriarity." He turned her name over on his tongue aloud. "A little long for lights. Or will you change it for professional purposes?"

"I don't think I'll change it," she said, rather shortly.

"A theatrical dynasty, of course," Duff murmured.

"If you're thinking of my father," Dinny said, lured to this subject in spite of herself, "I'm afraid he has always been pretty adequate." She looked sorry to have so spoken.

"That's a nasty remark, isn't it?" Duff said mildly. "Very damning."

She nodded. "I shouldn't have said that. I guess he's done all right, without ever making a splash. He's . . . Well, he's good. He's skillful."

"A good workman?"

"Yes, that's it. He's very versatile. Too versatile, maybe. He always likes to do something he's never done before. He was always restless."

"Not—what is it they call it?—typed?"

Dinny said, "I think he was scared of that. He keeps changing his name, starting over. He doesn't seem to stick, somehow."

"Keeps changing his name?"

"Oh, yes. My goodness, we never know."

Duff should have said, "Do you see him often?" It would have fallen in here, that casual question. Instead, he found himself looking away, looking at the dishes piled in the red wire drainer on the sink, thinking to himself that there seemed to be a lot of dishes.

He murmured, "So you slept well?"

"Oh, my goodness!" Dinny laughed. "I'll bet," she said gaily, "nobody told you anything about our ghost!"

Duff took a swallow of his coffee before he let his eyebrows soar in polite unbelief.

"We have one, you know. A Hessian. You know, one of those soldiers . . ."

"Yes," said Duff carefully, "go on."

"Well, the story is that he was one of those who ran away from the British Army. He didn't want to fight any more. He wanted to get food and shelter, so he asked here if they had any work. But I guess he couldn't speak English much. . . ."

"Here at this house?" said Duff without skepticism.

"Well, not this house, of course," she said. "This house isn't that old. But there was a house here then."

"During the American Revolution?"

"*Umhum*. Isn't it fascinating?"

"Very," said Duff. "He died here?"

"*Umhum*."

"And why doesn't he rest easy?"

"Oh." Dinny rolled her eyes. "Well, you see, all he wanted to do was work for his keep, kind of, but to the people who lived here he was one of the enemy. And they killed him, that night. They thought he was a spy. I guess that's why he doesn't rest. He . . . can't understand it yet."

"It must have been very disillusioning," Duff said.

"Well, of course it was." She giggled. "Anyhow, we hear things sometimes."

"Footsteps?"

"*Umhum*."

"Does he clank?"

"No-oo." Dinny said. "He moves around in the house."

"How does he like his eggs?" Duff said.

Dinny pushed back from the table with both hands on the edge of it. "What?"

But Duff's eyes grew dreamy. He settled back in his chair and looked past her while he talked. "Ah, that poor foreign boy," he said pulling out the emotional stops in his flexible voice, "who couldn't speak the language! I wonder if the propaganda got to him, the propaganda the patriots put out? Or I wonder if he simply felt it stirring in the air, the notion that must have been new to him, herded and sold as he was to fight a war for no reason of his, at all. I mean the notion that a man can stir his stumps and get out of that helpless herd and be for himself. Because here was a new kind of world, in which men didn't see why they shouldn't be and think and decide and work for themselves. An awfully new notion. But somehow or other, just such a notion that, once discovered, would keep gnawing and working in a man's head. Shouldn't you think so?

"Oh, I suppose they talked it over, in their own language, around their fires. And some said they would be damned if they weren't going to try it. I suppose he would have kept thinking about them, the ones who had gone, when the ranks closed up after them as if they had died in battle. But he would know they had not died, but had perhaps escaped."

Dinny was staring at him.

"So one night, he did it. He took the step, shook loose. Became a man instead of a statistic, a man with a private soul and some of his destiny in his hands. He must have been very much excited and afraid, too. After all, he was stepping into the unknown, and the risk was awful, like depending on there being a heaven, if you aren't sure. And he couldn't even talk about it. Because these people couldn't understand him. Poor foreign boy. He came to this door, ready to be friendly, ready to believe in miracles, perhaps in kindness and in help, or in the greater miracle of fair pay and no questions asked. And when he went to sleep that night, poor fellow, he did think it was going to be all right."

Duff's voice stopped, while he came back a hundred

and sixty-odd years. He smiled at Dinny. "You gave me a tragedy," he said. "Don't you think it's the essence of tragedy when what happens needn't have happened at all, had they been able to understand each other?"

Dinny swallowed. "I forgot you used to be a professor of American history."

"Oh, no. That you remembered," Duff said softly. "What you did forget"—he looked about as dreamy as a fox at this moment—"there's an old story about a woman who fell asleep in church and dreamed she was dying, and before she woke, she did die."

"But how did they know what she dreamed!" Dinny blurted and then kept her mouth open.

"Exactly. How did your folks know, after they'd killed him, that he *wasn't* a spy?" Duff waited for no answer. "My dear, it was sweet of you to make him a Hessian. You must know how fond I am of the Revolutionary period."

Dinny was looking down, and there was color in her face.

"Look here," Duff said, "you don't misunderstand me, do you? I am here as a friend, you know. Not quite as a spy." Dinny's eyes shot to his. "Have a conference," Duff suggested gently, "why don't you?"

And he went away.

He wandered out to the stable, which he found deserted. After some search, he located the place where the poisons were kept. It was an old cupboard that had been there when there were horses. It was secured by a small, very flimsy padlock, the key of which hung on a nail near by.

Duff opened it and examined the things he found.

111

Paper sacks with the name of their contents scrawled in pencil outside. A can or two. A bottle. Sinister names, of all the wrong poisons. Then he found a little cardboard box, covered with printing—40 per cent nicotine, and so forth. Here had been the right poison. Gone now. He knew Pring had taken it away. His fingers felt a paper inside the box, and he drew it out. Instructions for use. Ah, yes. Duff read them with very great interest and looked at all the pictures.

When he finally tucked the box back into the cupboard and locked it up again, he stood for a moment, running his eye over the garden tools, the rakes and hoes, the mower and the spade, the flower pots, the bags of fertilizer, the wheelbarrow, the hose, the pile of stakes, the clippers and trowels and dibble and pruning shears, hanging on the wall. And the sprayer, standing neatly in the corner.

It was a cylinder with a handle at the top with which one pumped up pressure. Then it could be slung over one's back and the spraying material released by the trigger at the end of the short, narrow hose. Duff was interested in the nozzle. He unscrewed its parts. There was a tiny screen inside, to turn a thin stream of liquid into a spray. The screen, however, was easily removable. Duff shook his head. Didn't know. Couldn't tell. Have to see the thing in action.

He didn't like the idea. Didn't like it at all. It seemed too pat and mechanical. It was very logical. It fitted so neatly. That was why he didn't like it.

The idea was that a harmless bottle of wine, standing on a table, could be made poisonous quickly in those very few possible minutes, by the boy who was just outside with a sprayer full of the right poison slung over his back at the time.

Davey would have seen. Perhaps Davey wouldn't tell or thought it was an elephant. But Alfie would have known. Alfie on the porch, calling, must have been a confederate. Paul would have had to come in through the French doors from the porch. He couldn't have put the sprayer through the window on the other side of the room because of the screen, or even if that had been raised, it was too far from the table. He would have had to cross a line of vision from the hall where the doctor and the victim were standing. Duff sighed. Not so logical, after all. Just startling, for a moment. Surely the stuff was diluted almost to nothing in this sprayer, according to instructions. Must have been. He must ask to see the toxicologist's report, he thought.

Approaching the house, he heard, through its opened windows, a joyous commotion. "Hey, Taffy's home!" Davey and Mitch ran shrieking across the terrace, and the garden door banged after them. Upstairs, Dinny's voice called it out. "Taffy's home!" He could hear the boys thumping down the stairs from their lair. "Taffy's home!"

He himself got indoors soon enough to see Taffy, pinched into a stretcher by grinning ambulance men, ride triumphantly, to shouts of joy, up the stairs at home.

Mary had come in behind. She stood in her own house and sighed and pushed her hand through her hair. Duff went toward her, smiling. "How is she?"

"She's full of beans!" said Mary. "Oh, she's fine." Her eyes slid into the living room and grazed the red couch. "Everything looks all right here. They haven't been a trouble to you, have they?"

So confidently did she expect him to say, "Oh, no, of course not," that she was halfway up the stairs and still smiling when she realized that Duff had said, "Oh, yes, of course." She stopped and threw him a puzzled but not worried look, and went on to settle Taffy.

Duff felt just a little forlorn. The house to keep, the kids to watch. . . . Now these were Mary's. Mary looked better. She was almost pretty. Certainly attractive. Rested, now. What a nice straight body. She seemed young. Living with these kids would keep you young. Have to look sharp. No doubt she did. Intelligent. And what loving unity . . . damn' nice bunch of kids . . . she was the core, the source . . .

Duff caught his mind whipping about like a flag in the wind and stilled and steadied it, deliberately.

In some ways, he realized, this was being and going to be his most difficult case, because he was not thinking, not seeing, not hearing quite clearly. Everything passed through a blurring personal emotion. His own emotion. He, MacDougal Duff, caught by feelings in the matter. He would have to spy them out and weigh them and then discount them, these feelings, whatever they were. He was involved. Because he was afraid for Taffy, yes, and sorry for Mary, and envious, touched, concerned . . .

He'd better, he told himself sternly, cracking the slang like a whip over his seething insides, he'd better pull himself together.

CHAPTER 9

The men with the stretcher came down again, and
Duff, standing in the front door, watching the
ambulance back out of the drive, became aware of Dr.
Christenson's car pulled up at the curb and of the
doctor himself talking very earnestly to a rather
dapper-looking fellow whom Duff had not seen before.
Pricked by curiosity which, in his business, was so often
a part of his duty, Duff went out and strolled down the
walk toward them.

The doctor's friend was a slight man, of medium
height, with a narrow chest which he seemed to be
trying to puff out. He stood with his shoulder blades
drawn together in the back and his chin drawn in.
Hatless, in summer slacks and a shirt open at the neck,
he nevertheless looked dapper. Dark-haired, blue-
chinned, his face wizened and lined, and yet not old, he

turned weak gray eyes on Duff without seeming to see him at all.

"Good morning," said the doctor. "Mr. O'Leary, Mr. Duff."

Duff took a thin hand that squeezed his with convulsive strength. He saw in O'Leary's other hand an object something like a watch. He said, "I believe I have spoken to Mr. O'Leary on the phone."

O'Leary cocked his head. "Oh, yes. Yes, of course. Last night, wasn't it?" It was not so much the turn of the vowels that gave that British effect as the rise and fall and the quick pace of the voice.

"I wish you would tell me," Duff said, "because I've been bothered ever since. Why on earth did you call me Professor Moriarity?"

The man's eyes moved impatiently. "That's simple enough. After all, the doctor told me he would be at the Moriarity house."

"But why Professor?"

"Oh, I don't know. It seemed very natural, somehow. Don't you think so?"

"If the doctor had been at the Brown house, you'd have asked for Father?"

"Father Brown? Yes, that does sound familiar, too. Doesn't it?" O'Leary bobbed his head at them. He put the thing that looked like a watch into his shirt pocket. "Er . . . five miles then. See you later." He set off down the sidewalk with shoulder blades still drawn together and his feet doing a nimble heel-and-toe.

"What's the matter with him?" Duff asked.

"Nerves," said Dr. Christenson shortly.

"You say he is staying with you?"

"Yes." The doctor sighed heavily. "*I* don't know. Queer fellow. How's Taffy?"

They went up to see Taffy together.

She was enthroned in her own bed holding court for all of her brothers and sisters. Taffy's eyes were bright and her face was merry. Her pretty mouth and teeth looked as if they had been born smiling. She wore thick taffy-colored pigtails, pulled away from a center part, but the fair hair escaped in little wispy curls around her forehead. She looked, Duff thought, as happy as a little lark. And so, indeed, did everyone look happy.

"Are you going to telephone to my tummy again?" she demanded of the doctor. The doctor said yes, he was, and used his stethoscope. Taffy giggled some and then breathed for him, all obedience and sober co-operation. The doctor tweaked the end of her nose and said he guessed she wasn't sick any more.

Paul said, "Hey, Taffy, how was the hospital?"

Alfie said, "Did they wind the bed up and down for you?"

"It folded up," said Taffy, "something like a W." She spoke slowly without slurring at all. The effect was grave and charming.

"But what did it do?" Davey demanded. Paul began to demonstrate with a strip of paper.

Duff withdrew with Mary and the doctor. It was a scene so far from death, so far from murder, so far from evil, that it made the throat ache.

They went down to the living room, and Mary looked around as if her housewife's eye saw work ahead, and then she sighed and said, "Well, I suppose I'd better keep her down a day or two?"

117

"Yes," said the doctor, "if you can."

"You look tired," Mary said. "Have you time for a cup of coffee?" Her eyes were drawn to the windows and the garden. "Let's have some outside."

So Duff and the doctor found themselves lying in long wooden chairs in flickering shade, looking across the roses to where a green peninsula of lawn tongued into the shrubbery, flowed around a little pool, and reunited to meet a white gate under the trees. The red roof of a house was partly visible.

"Eve's house." The doctor nodded. He put a cigarette into the holder he affected. "Mary's garden is lovely, isn't it? She works very hard on it."

"Yes, it's lovely," Duff said.

"Connie's rather let her flowers go."

"Miss Avery has a farm, they tell me."

"Well, a small farm. Yes, I suppose it is a farm. A beautiful place. On the water front, you see. Valuable land. Belonged to her father, of course. Now it's Connie's, since her mother prefers the city now, in her old age. Connie's father—er—" The doctor didn't finish, but Duff knew it would have been something rapturous. "I'm pretty lucky," the doctor admitted, "and for the life of me, I don't know why."

"A very handsome young woman," Duff murmured, hoping this would do.

"Yes, isn't she? Yes, something distinguished about her. It's not only her looks"—the doctor was very earnest about it—"it's everything. Character, intelligence, and she's very capable, very strong, really. Very fine," he added reverently.

"She raises chickens?" Duff managed not to prick

the balloon, though well he might have with such an incongruous and earthy remark.

"Oh, yes, since the war. She knows a great deal about—er—breeding, that sort of thing. Has kennels, you see. At first it was a hobby, but I do believe that she can show a little profit on her dogs. Lovely animals. They're rather famous. Miss Avery's Irish setters. Of course, she's only begun with chickens."

"Chickens must be rather a let-down," Duff mused. "Aren't they . . . rather filthy? Have to be deloused and all that?"

The doctor turned his head and a wandering sun-ray flashed on his glasses, obscuring Duff's sight of his eyes. Duff went on, "But I suppose she has farmhands to do all that sort of thing."

"Naturally," the doctor said rather sharply. "And so do dogs have to be defleaed, you know."

"But not with nicotine," drawled Duff.

The doctor pulled his feet off the footrest and seemed crouched to spring up. "Look here," he said fiercely, "what are you trying to get at?"

"I've been reading the folder that comes with nicotine sulphate," Duff said mildly, his voice making no emphasis or comment. "I see it is recommended for painting roosts. Ah, well, learn something every day." He looked slumbrous, but the doctor was not comforted.

"Let me put you straight," he snapped. "Constance Avery never saw Emily Brown in her life, never knew her, never had anything to do with her, and I daresay that if it weren't for my knowing her, Constance wouldn't care whether she lived or died."

119

"I'm sure not," Duff murmured.

"Furthermore, she was not in or near this house since Brownie came, and could not possibly . . ."

Duff raised a brow.

"Not possibly!" the doctor shouted.

"Did you think I was accusing her?"

"You couldn't do that," the doctor said heavily. He pulled his handkerchief out of his pocket, and a cardboard pierced with bobby pins came out and fell to the flagstones. Duff made a little gesture to indicate them, and the doctor picked them up. Brass, they were. For butter-colored hair.

Duff said, raising his hand as if to apologize before he spoke.

"How old is Miss Avery, doctor?"

"Miss Avery is thirty-five," the doctor told him defiantly. "She wouldn't mind your knowing that, since she doesn't mind its being known, or I wouldn't tell you."

"My dear fellow," said Duff gently, "what are you defending so fiercely? It occurred to me to wonder, that's all. Has she been married before?"

"No," the doctor said, seeming mollified. "No."

"Surely she's had many suitors?"

"Many. But her standards are very high. That's why," the doctor added simply, taking all the vanity out of his previous remark, "I can't believe, sometimes, that she has chosen me."

Duff was muttering something about happiness when Mary came out with the coffee.

It was good coffee, and the garden was very lovely. Duff hated to strike at the peace and the beauty of this place. The doctor struck first.

"So it was nicotine," he said. "I wish I'd known. Something might have been done for her if I had known. Though it was pretty fast, pretty quickly too late."

"You had the results of the tests this morning?"

"Yes. I spoke to Dr. Surf. He . . . they don't seem to—er—" The doctor dropped his remark in the middle again.

"No," said Duff, "they don't seem to have come to any conclusion about what happened. Neither have I."

Mary put her cup down. "Do they think that the poison came from here, from my things in the stable?"

"They don't know," Duff told her. "Nicotine is not used in medicine, is it, doctor?"

"No," the doctor said, "no."

"But it is not difficult to buy? No obstacles?"

"I shouldn't think so."

"Where do you get yours, Mary?"

"From the place where I get my fertilizers," she said. "You can order it from garden catalogues, too. You can get it in hardware stores, even the dime store. Of course, there's a skull and crossbones on it." Her shoulders shook.

"Is it good for roses?"

"For lots of things. Roses? Yes." Mary swallowed. "Paul was using some yesterday. Very much diluted."

"So I understand," said Duff casually.

Sun was on the doctor's glasses again. He put his cup down and rose to leave. "Not Paul," he said firmly. "Don't think of it. Must have been an accident, of course. Don't you think so, Mr. Duff? Really?"

"Perhaps," Duff said. "We certainly do not *know* that it *wasn't* an accident . . . do we?"

The doctor didn't answer. He stood still a moment, and then started abruptly off. Mary followed him as far as the garden door.

When she came drifting back, Duff assumed by his manner that they would go on sitting here. He hoped they would. He said, "The good doctor is pretty rapturous about his fiancee, isn't he? She was here last night, you know."

"Oh, she did come?" Mary sat down. "How did you like her?"

Duff said very carefully. "I'm not sure. For one thing, she struck me as the real thing in a snob."

"Oh, well, she can't help that," Mary said, twinkling. "Old family, old money, blue blood, you know. Her mother was one of the Van der Hoorsts."

"Whereas, *my* mother was one of the Mulligans," Duff said.

Mary began to laugh. When she laughed she looked a little like Taffy. There was a fleeting impression of that laughing little girl.

"I'll tell you," she said. "It's one of those family things. And it's about Constance. You see, when she and Norry got engaged, I threw them a party. That was last March. Well, we have a nice fat lady who comes and does for us when there's too much for me to handle. She's Irish. We've known her for ages—ever since servants went out of the world, anyhow. But I think she only comes to us.

"Anyway, she was passing trays, hors d'oeuvres and sandwiches. She was in and around, and all the while Constance was holding forth about family. It was a little bit thick, too. Everyone had to trot out a pedigree for Constance to inspect and hear that *her* mother was one of the Van der Hoorsts. It got to be a refrain. Of course, that's Constance, and I didn't think much about it. But what happened! When Constance was about to take her—uh—royal departure"—Mary had a thin dimple—"she took it into her head to say gracious words to Maggie. She said . . . something like . . . 'You served that very nicely.' "

Mary was a good mimic. Duff could hear the "my good woman" air of it.

"And Maggie! Maggie reared back and said"—Mary rolled out the brogue—" 'And why wouldn't I, Miss Avery? Me mother was one of the Mulligans!' "

Mirth belonged in this garden; the sun and the dirty coffee cups and the laughter were all part of its delight. How delightful it was to him, MacDougal Duff, stretched out long in the chair, laughing like a boy, didn't dare admit.

But Paul, mooching along out of the house with a bun in his hand, demanding to know what the joke was, sobered them. Mary told him what the joke was, old stuff to Paul, and he put a pillow on the flagstones, sat down there, and leaned his back against a tree. He ate his bun, while Duff and Mary Moriarity looked off across the garden and remembered how MacDougal Duff came to be here.

Mary said, "Tell me what they think, will you?" So Duff told her about the poison and the wine and the fingerprints and about Eve.

She drew in her breath at that, but made no comment.

When he had finished, Paul, who had been listening with his head bowed over his knees, sat up straight and began to talk.

"The thing is, Mom, don't you see, whether or not you drank that wine Dinny put on your tray."

"Why?" she said. She looked at her big son as if she were willing to let him lead.

"You haven't asked her yet?" Paul said to Duff.

"I haven't asked her anything."

"Well, then, that's going to be the thing. Because, the way it is now, it's this way. If you *didn't* drink the wine, then maybe that bottle was poisoned all the time. Nobody else had any wine out of it—or anyhow not since earlier in the afternoon."

"Not even then," said Duff. "Or at least not necessarily."

"Yeah, I mean, so far as we know. So, if you *didn't* drink it, then that throws the thing wide open. The poison could have been put in there any time, and all we have to do is figure out how it got on the table when it did. And maybe Mitch did that, no matter what she says. Of course, she didn't know it was poisoned." Paul stopped and looked at Duff, who nodded.

"O.K." Paul went on. "But if you *did* drink it, then the only way it could have happened was that somebody put the poison in there later, in just that little while when Brownie was gone and Alfie was gone and Dinny was upstairs and Mitch was in the kitchen. So it couldn't have been, for instance, Taffy."

Mary bit her lip suddenly.

"Or . . . or you." Paul said. "Or Dinny, I guess."

"Not so," Duff said. "You may as well keep it perfectly straight. It could have been Dinny."

"Well, anyhow. . . . Whoever put the poison in could have changed the places of the bottles, too. For instance, maybe he put it in the one in the pantry, just because it *was* in the pantry and he couldn't be seen fooling around with it in there. Then he could have switched them, quick. It wouldn't take a minute."

"Under Davey's nose?" Duff asked.

"Sure. Davey's pretty small." Paul scratched his ankles vigorously "So you see, Mom?" Then to Duff, "Aren't you going to ask her?"

"I think she'll tell us," Duff said.

Mary's eyes flickered. Then she looked up across the roses. "But I *did* drink it," she said. "I was worried about Taffy and tired. I even thought maybe the doctor had sent it up for me. So, of course, I drank it." Her eyes settled on Paul, and she smiled.

He didn't smile back, although the understanding between them was almost tangible. "You didn't have two bottles of that stuff, did you, Mom?" he said. "Only my fingerprints are on the one that was out there."

"Proving?" Duff asked.

"Well, probably the poison never belonged to us," Paul said. "Because, naturally, I didn't do it."

The white gate at the end of the lawn flew open, and Eve Meredith's thin, hurrying figure came, in her anxious hobble, toward them.

"Mary, you're home! Is Taffy all right then?" She gave Duff a jerk of her head. She looked a little less raddled today in a green summer dress, with red sandals on her thin feet.

"Taffy's fine," said Mary.

"Oh, Lord!" Eve dumped herself into a chair.

125

"Those detectives! Those men! They've been in my house for hours. I think they think I did it."

Duff studied her. She didn't seem horrified by her own conclusions. She had an air of considering this preposterous.

"They took my fingerprints," said Eve with a snort that might have meant amusement, "and it seems my fingerprints are on that poisoned wine bottle."

Duff met Paul's eyes.

"Of all things!" Eve rattled. "I told them, of course they were. It was my wine. And I gave it to her. Naturally, I touched it! But it wasn't poisoned when I gave it to her. I'm sure of that."

Paul said aside to Duff, "Dinny's too, weren't they?"

Duff nodded. "Yes, so it would seem. We conclude that it was Mrs. Meredith's wine standing in the pantry. Mrs. Meredith's wine poured out by Dinny for her mother. Mrs. Meredith's wine subsequently got poisoned and transported to the dining room and into Brownie's glass. It was not," he said to Eve, "poisoned when you gave it to her."

"That's what I *said*," she said.

Paul squirmed. "Unless Dinny might've messed around with both bottles . . ."

"Or unless your mother *didn't* drink her wine, after all."

"But I did!" said Mary.

"And Dinny didn't!" said Dinny indignantly behind them. "What goes on out here? Mother, what's for lunch?"

Mary started to get out of her chair, but Paul was up and pushed her back. "I'll help Dinny," he said very gruffly. "Come on, Din. We'll dig up something."

126

"Yeah, sandwiches!" Dinny jeered.

"What's the matter with sandwiches?"

"Nothing's the matter with sandwiches except they're practically all bread!"

"What's the matter with bread?"

The children disappeared. Mary was smiling. She gave Duff a little glance well tinged with pride.

CHAPTER 10

Just the same," said Eve, quite as if no one had spoken in between, "I'm going to go in for rotenone after this. They asked me if I had any of the stuff. Well, of course I have. But I don't think, I honestly don't think I can bear to use nicotine any more."

"Have you heard from Ralph?" asked Mary.

"No, no, nothing. But it's terrifying!" Eve, apparently, was not diverted. "I knew it was a poison, but not like I know it now. To think we've been fooling around with that stuff for years and thinking nothing of it!"

Mary said, "How *is* the war, anyhow? Was there any news in the paper this morning?"

But Eve was deep in local horrors and would not be turned away. "Bad enough to think of swallowing it!" she cried. "But worse than that, it can go right through your skin! Did you know that? Did you know it can make you sick just if it gets on you?" Her reddish-brown eyes went down to her hands, and her fingers writhed.

"Oh, Eve, don't," begged Mary. "Don't keep it in your mind. Besides, you know perfectly well that if you get aphis . . ."

"No. I'll try rotenone," Eve said stubbornly.

"Mommy . . . Mommy . . ." Out of the window in the wing above them came Mitch's black head. "Taffy wants to go to the bathroom." Davey's head popped out beside her. "Taffy wants . . ."

"Pull that screen *down*," said Mary. She got up and whisked into the house.

Eve's fingers were still writhing. Thin white hands, she had. "I'm so glad Taffy's all right again. Isn't it amazing how quickly they get well, those little things? But I'm so glad. Mr. Duff, you are a detective, aren't you?"

"I am," he said. He added nothing, but sat very quietly waiting. He felt she was winding up for an explosion. He hoped it would be a bombshell of information. He lay low, because he didn't know how to guide her toward it. His silence might do best.

Eve said, "I'm so sorry for Mary. So awfully sorry." She squirmed in her chair. "Such a terrible thing!" She clutched her own throat. "In her house, like that! I should think it would just make them want to move out."

She was slipping off. Duff gave a little push. He said, "At least Taffy's better." He wanted to turn her back to Taffy.

"I wonder what made her sick?" Eve said in a thick voice, as if it were being forced out of her by interior
129

pressure. "What made Taffy sick, I wonder?"

Duff said, "Doesn't the doctor know?" But this was wrong. He knew he had made a mistake as soon as the words were out. Eve boiled over into a spate of explanation with the effect of having found a safety valve.

"Oh, it's almost impossible to know about little children. I mean, you can't possibly be sure. They play. Who knows what they get into? Why, it could be any one of a dozen things. Who knows what they pick up and put in their mouths? Or what germs other children might be carrying? Sometimes you never find out. All you can do is be glad when they're better. I can remember . . ."

Duff said, "I understand you have a son, Mrs. Meredith. In the service? Would that be Ralph?"

"Yes," she said. "Yes, that's my boy. Nineteen years old. It's too young, Mr. Duff. Too young!" She pounded the chair with her fist.

"If you were nineteen, you wouldn't think so," Duff told her. "We forget, I think."

"I suppose that's true." She looked surprised.

"When you were nineteen, did you think of yourself as a child? I'm sure you didn't. That is, if you can really remember."

"I was . . . Oh, my God, I was married and pregnant . . ." Eve looked, for the first time, thoughtful and therefore nearly serene.

"Your husband died?" Duff wondered.

"He could be dead now," she said roughly, "for all I know."

"Divorce?"

130

"Oh, yes," she said. "He divorced me, finally." Her fingers were twisting again. One hand gripped the other until the knuckles cracked. "So he's *my* boy," she said. "Because Edgar gave him up. Afterwards, he never had any right to him. He was afraid. Well, I wasn't afraid. But if they"—she sobbed a dry sob as if her heart tore—"if they hurt him now, well, it's all I've lived for. Ralph. If they hurt him, that's the end of me. The end! The end!"

She pounded again. Duff leaned over and stopped her frantic hand. "It's very hard," he said, "but you can't hold him safe by stretching your nerves until they break. Give him up a little. It might be better for him."

He felt her hand loosen. "You mean, what I fear will come upon me?" she whispered superstitiously. "Do you believe that?"

Duff said, rather lightly, "You wouldn't walk under a ladder, would you? Just in case . . ." He leaned back. "Tell me what your husband was afraid of."

Eve's face, that had been loosened and wondering, tightened up again. "You ought to stick with what's your own," she said bitterly. "I don't blame *her*. Oh, of course, I do blame her. Did blame her. She had no business telling him things. No business, no excuse at all. Even if she thought he knew it." Her thick voice poured scorn. "But she never thought he knew it. She knew he didn't know it. She knew damn' well. Oh, I blamed *her*, all right. Just for fun, just to stick her oar in, just to make an effect . . . What did it mean to her? Not a thing. It meant plenty to me, but she never thought of that. She wouldn't.

"But I blame him. I blame him more. All it proves is

131

that he was no good. Cowardly. He couldn't stick. Well, good riddance! I thank God it meant he never wanted Ralph. Ralph's been all mine."

Duff said craftily, "How did Miss Brown know?"

"I've got a cousin in California," Eve said viciously. "Or had."

"This cousin told Miss Brown. Miss Brown told your husband." Duff seemed to be musing aloud. "It was something about your family."

Eve made a gesture of finality. "Just a story," she said.

"Not even true?"

Her auburn eyes had narrowed in. "Of course it wasn't true," she said in another voice, a voice that was no longer strangled and tortured as it came from her throat. A lighter, shrill, metallic voice. "Anyhow, that was years ago." Her laugh clanged. "Why, I've been a grass widow longer than Mary . . ."

Mary was coming back. "I think," she said, "that the kids are about to produce food. You'll stay, won't you, Eve?"

"No," said Eve. "No, I can't, Mary. I shouldn't, really. I've got to go downtown. I'll be over later. Later." She got up and took herself away with that nervous awkwardness of hers. Duff watched her across the grass, her huddled posture, her quick cramped step, the way she drove her heels.

"Poor Eve," said Mary, echoing his thought. "Poor Eve."

"Tell me the story of her life," Duff said. "Please. What was it Brownie did? What was it she told?"

Mary looked straight at him with her very blue eyes.

"I don't know anything about it but a rumor," she said frankly. "Eve dodges away from telling me, and I've never directly asked her. Brownie never said, and I never asked her, either. It wasn't any of my business. It's not my business now." She stopped speaking but kept her eyes steady.

Duff's were just as steady. "Nevertheless," he said, "you know the rumor, and the rumor is what I want. You have scruples about telling because, I suspect, although she says not, the story *was* true. And the rumor is the story. You say it's none of your business. If and when I show you that it *is* your business, you will tell me, won't you?"

Mary looked startled and a good deal less sure of herself. "Why," she said, "how could it be my business?"

But Duff looked away and gloomily down at his well-shod feet. "Other people's business," he muttered. "I daresay it would be very pleasant to mind only your own. And yet, since it is *my* business to poke and pry and snoop—"

Mary said quickly, "I know."

"I ask questions," said Duff, "that I *must* ask. There are times when I don't enjoy it."

"Please ask me anything you'd like," said Mary in distress. "Anything I can tell you, about my own business, you know I will. You know I want—"

"I don't want to ask *you* any questions at all," Duff said. "Not you."

His long hands were lying still on the arms of the chair, still from old habit. But he thought: If this goes on, I'll be twisting them like Eve. Aside from that, his mind felt vacant, as if the conversation had come to a jumping-off-place. There wasn't any solid ground on which to proceed. The silence seemed to quiver.

Mary said dreamily, "Do you see that rosebush, over there? The pink and white striped roses? Those quaint little old-fashioned ones? That's Taffy's rose. I put it in the year she was born. Rosa Mundi."

"It's not like Taffy," Duff said. "Too fussy. Taffy's got a pure line, like those—what do you call them?—those real roses."

"Hybrid teas," said Mary. "Mr. Duff, what can I tell you that will help us?"

Duff felt his heart jump. He pushed this remarkable sensation down in his consciousness, to be considered later. He ground his teeth.

"Had your husband," he said, between them, "what is known as a sense of humor?"

Mary looked bewildered. Her face puckered up to laugh, and then she didn't laugh. "Oh, yes," she said solemnly, "Yes, he had."

"He was, I suppose, one of those handsome rascals," growled MacDougal Duff.

Mary looked very queer. Then her face settled into a sober mask. "That's about right," she said quietly.

Duff stared at a red, red rose. A black pall seemed to have settled over the garden. If Moriarity was in the house, or had been, did she know it yet? Had the kids told her, just now? How would she react? What, in God's name, did the fellow mean to her?

Duff made a mighty effort. He smiled. "Was Brownie worried about growing old? Did she mind gray hair?"

Mary simply stared.

"Oh, never mind," he said. "Do you know, I'm afraid this business of mine leads to all kinds of lurid speculation. I think of the darnedest things. Forgive me."

Mary looked very demure, somehow.

"But we've got to get down to it," Duff said sadly. "Tell me about breakfast yesterday morning and what you said to the kids, Mary."

Mary gasped. She put her hand over her eyes.

"Your kids are wonderful," Duff said, "but we've got to know what we are afraid of. Will it help you to trust me if I tell you I've fallen pretty hard for your children? They have my affection . . . friendship . . . love," he said.

Mary looked at him with frightened eyes. "But you know," she wailed, "you just don't *say* to your children, 'Now, darlings, remember we ought not to go around killing people. Mind you don't commit any murders or Mama s-spank.'" Her voice broke. "Oh, I don't believe it!" she cried. "I don't really believe it, you know."

"Of course you don't believe it," said Duff stoutly.

"But you bear them and you raise them, and all of a sudden they're people. They've got their own differences. They're not little copies of you. They aren't your duplicates, your children aren't. The chromosomes or whatever they are have been shuffled. It's a new deal, a new creature. You can't prophesy. You can't *know*. And if I—"

"Hush," said Duff. "Naturally, you're worried. Tell me what you said yesterday morning."

Mary sniffed loudly and tried to smile. "Oh, Brownie was in one of her stern moods. You know she has our mortgage, my mortgage?" Duff nodded. "Well,

135

she just all of a sudden began to complain about the high cost of living and all that, and she wanted quite a lot of money. Some of it I owed her, and some I didn't owe her yet. But what can you say? I said I'd do the best I could, but we live, too, and it costs *us* more. I was upset. She'd said all this Saturday night. I worried all night long. She didn't come down early to breakfast, and I'm afraid I passed my worry on to the children.

"It's something I . . . sometimes do," said Mary. "They know how we live. The money is partly a settlement from Denis, partly my own. It's not much, either. They know all about it so that they'll understand when they can't have things they want. And they do understand. They're wonderful.

"What I said was, 'Brownie's cracking down. Lord, I wish she wouldn't, right now.'" Mary was quoting herself, trying to be accurate. "The boys thought that was being mean. I said, 'Maybe she can't help it, but I can't help it, either. I haven't got the money.' Taffy said, 'What money, Mommy?' I said, 'Money Brownie wants, dear. Maybe we'll have to go away from this house.' Mitch yowled. Davey was all ready to yowl, too. So I said, 'Maybe not. Maybe she'll up and die and leave us her fortune. Pass the sugar.'" Mary stopped. Then she added with painful honesty, "One of them said, 'I wish she would.'"

"Which one?"

"T-taffy." Mary swallowed hard. "But then I made light of the whole thing. I thought I'd erased it."

Duff said, "That's not very significant. You worry most about Taffy, don't you?"

"I don't know why," Mary wailed. "But she's so exquisite . . . that pure line, you said. She's so serious

136

and precise and h-happy. We . . . we all adore her so. I mean, we've never had to scold her. So I wonder if she'd know . . . b-better? How could she know better? I keep wondering . . . And besides, she was so sick . . . she was feverish . . . maybe——"

"Don't cry," Duff said. "My God, I know how you want to cry. It's terrifying. I've never been so frightened at anything in my life. But if that's all . . . and it *is* all?"

She looked at him wonderingly.

"Then cheer up," he said. "Nothing's going to happen to Taffy. I'll see that it doesn't. I promise you."

Mary didn't say, "You're so good, you're so kind." She threw herself on his mercy, into his heart. She said, "Oh, please see that it doesn't, Mr. Duff. Please do."

"Have you . . . asked her, Mary?"

Mary put her face in her hands. "I can't."

"Hey, Mom . . ." It was Alfie, singing out through the living-room window. "Somebody to see-ee you." They could see his pale hair close to the screen. He made a megaphone out of his hands and added in a hoarse romantic whisper, "It's the cops."

Mary blew her nose hard in a scrap of handkerchief. She said clearly, "Bring them out here, dear."

Duff sat back and watched her stiffen herself, become a gracious lady, and handle them. She seemed to him to be just right—straightforward, definite but not too definite, friendly, neither cheerful nor sad, she answered their questions. He felt that the starch must go out of them as she spoke. He thought he could feel them relaxing. He, himself, sat quietly by, and it was

137

not until later that he realized what he might have seemed to be doing.

Actually, he was watching Mary's face, thinking that her nose was definitely too long, her face a little too narrow, her dark hair not very neat, her eyebrows too level and unarched, and yet she was a fine-looking woman, a very attractive woman, a woman of great charm. And if Paul was fifteen, then Mary must be between thirty-five and forty, perhaps . . .

Yes, Mary was saying, the little girl had been taken sick in the afternoon, about three or a little after, and she had asked Miss Brown to go next door for the ice collar. Yes, Miss Brown had gone and returned with it, and if she had also brought back a bottle of wine, Mary had not known that. She, herself, had been busy with the little girl. Yes, all the time. Until she had heard screaming, and her oldest daughter had come running up to tell her.

She had been with the stricken woman and the doctor, of course, until she had died. Then the doctor had suggested the hospital. Mary had gone upstairs to reassure the children, get the little one ready. Yes, certainly, she had drunk the wine on her tray.

No, she had not gone into the dining room at any time. Nor turned off any toaster.

It was Pring who remembered to ask that. It was Robin who added, aside to Duff, that he had found no one among the technicians who knew anything about turning off the toaster.

Mary went on. Yes, Miss Brown had held her mortgage. She was an old friend and, of course, friends with Mary's friends, here in New Rochelle. No, she knew of no enemies. Mrs. Meredith? Well, that was a longstanding thing. They hadn't liked each other as girls. Mrs. Meredith was an intense kind of person. Very much worried just now about her boy. In Mary's opinion, she would hardly . . .

The poison? Oh, no, the garden chemicals and poisons were never brought into the house. She had tried to be careful. They were kept locked out of anyone's careless reach. As far as she could remember, there had been only one container of nicotine sulphate out there.

It was a dreadful thing to have happened. Mary couldn't explain it. She said she hoped very much that they would be able to explain it. She didn't like people dying of poison in her house.

Pring pretty near patted her hand. "Now," he said, "don't worry." He thanked her. Robin thanked her.

They got up to go and brought Duff out of his chair to show them back through the house, to the door.

"How did you make out with Mrs. Meredith?" he asked them.

"We took it easy." Pring shrugged. He looked a bit resentful. "She's on wires, all right. But I don't think she did it. Just didn't like the dame. Never had liked her. Well, what would she up and poison her for? Hell, she laid herself right open if she did. How could she know we'd get balled up with the wine bottles?"

"True," Duff said. "I'm beginning to wonder if anyone did it."

Robin shifted his cud of gum. "Accident. What *I* say . . . The bottle the Meredith dame had . . . Listen, it was standing open around her house for days. She's had two, three different cleaning women in and out. Who knows what mighta happened?" His shrug was massive.

"Yeah, only Mrs. Moriarity says she *drank* some of that wine," said Pring irritably. "Well,"—his somber gaze searched Duff's face—"they're gonna bury her tomorrow. The inquest's put off till Friday. You got anything?"

Duff, whose heart was heavy, did his best. He said, "I haven't got a damn' thing. You know more about these people than I do." He kicked the carpet and looked annoyed and glum and a bit hostile. He was trying to look like a baffled man.

He sensed that they did not, now, wish to suspect Mary. Certainly they were not much impressed with the case against Mrs. Meredith. The thought of the children had not crossed their minds. He hoped grimly it never would. Actually, he realized, they were willing to go along with an accident theory if they could find one. They had a piece of an accident theory all ready.

The trouble, the hitch, the obstacle to this comfortable solution was their suspicion of himself. Not as a murderer, but as one who turned up where murder was. He had, so far, done more harm than good. Much more.

Probably if he had not walked in and announced that he was going to handle this case for Mrs. Moriarity, the accident theory would have unrolled smoothly, as the obvious thing. After all, it was the devil to prove one of these poison cases when the poison was so easy to get hold of. They would have shrugged it off. Accident. Too bad. The leader of the Boy Scouts would have made speeches to his troops re carelessness in the home. Maybe the Mayor would proclaim a Safety Week. Dreadful thing. Just goes to show. Did you hear about that woman . . . ?

Oh, they would have buried Brownie.

Also, if Duff had not held forth to the kids about these wine bottles, would Paul have presented his careful "either, or" to his mother this morning? Would Mary have seen, so clearly, the significance of the wine on her tray?

Then would she have said she drank it?

Duff didn't dare point out to Pring the possibility that she had lied. Nor the fact of the time, the very short time, in which she claimed to have gulped it down. For Dinny went up while the doctor and Miss Brown stood in the hall. Dinny was on her way down when the scream came. How long was that? Had Dinny lingered upstairs? No, Alfie's evidence made the time short. Mary was claiming to have taken the wine in one gulp. Had Mary eaten what was on her tray? "The toast was bitten . . ."

Duff groaned to himself.

He couldn't tell them Mary might have lied. To make Taffy safe. Of course. If she had lied, that was why. But he couldn't undermine their faith in her evidence, even to clear the way, now, for the accident theory.

And he couldn't, now, erase the scene on the terrace or the impression he must have made, staring at Mary so, as if he, with his damned reputation, had been doubting her.

His damned reputation. And he, standing here like a fool, trying to look baffled, thought to undermine *that* in this moment.

He said he would run down to headquarters after lunch and look at the toxicologist's report, if they didn't mind. They said they didn't mind, and went away.

Committed to saving Taffy, no matter what, even if it meant obscuring the truth, wretched in the conviction that he was standing, instead, squarely in the way of the easy way out, Duff drifted into the little music room and stood, staring down at the piano keys. This room was dim and quiet. But all around, behind him and above, ran the life of the house, the sunny life, the cheerful sounds. Perhaps he ought to go away, back to his own place. He was a bird of ill omen, a raven, a croaker. They would have been all right.

Duff shook himself. He let out his tension, let his worries go. Long, limp, he pulled his trick of letting himself fall apart, to come to rest in a safer place. He listened. He waited. All that came was the conviction that he, himself, must know what the truth was before he could do anything about it, even suppress it.

They called him to lunch, and he went.

But he had done himself good, after all. His mind seemed to have recovered its equilibrium, and he found himself able to study these children, out here on the terrace among the sandwiches and the lemonade, with a semblance of objectivity. Everyone was there except Taffy and Davey, who had refused to leave the bedside. Those two were having a picnic upstairs.

Duff considered Dinny, the actress, the taker of roles, the dark-eyed one. But there could be no possible doubt about Dinny. Never in the world would she have done it. Duff could well imagine her brushing aside the letter of the truth if she thought it would help protect Taffy, or anyone she loved. That she was capable of doing and doing well. A romantic role. Oh, yes. This role she might even play without there being any need for her to play it

But not the deed itself. Not murder. She was too . . . too what? Too essentially sweet and unviolent. Too—he groped for words to express his feeling—too important. Too dedicated a child to smear up her life with the death of so unimportant a person as Miss Emily Brown.

Paul? There was a clear head, an organizing intelligence. Duff tried not to wince at the conviction that if Paul wished to commit a murder he would do it very efficiently indeed. But he, too, was not violent. Not even impulsive. He especially adored his little sister Taffy. True, he had resented something Brownie had done to her. He had not cared for Brownie. But the boy was grown, was solid, reliable, and of all of them the most committed to civilization and order.

Duff looked at Alfie, whose cheerful face was so deceptively happy-go-lucky. Alfie was alert, liked excitement, adventure. Alfie was stuffed with yarns about detectives and, no doubt, G-men and modern Robin Hoods. Could he have mixed up fantasy and reality? He was younger than Paul, and in a way younger than Dinny, his twin. Could he have committed murder for romantic reasons, to save the old homestead? Nonsense! No. Alfie was up to something, all right. He wasn't as smooth as Dinny was about hiding it. Or as Paul, who hid it by not being excited about it at all. They were all up to something. Still, he couldn't think that what they were up to was the murder itself.

Mitch? Well, now, Mitch. One didn't get at Mitch.

Eleven years old. Changing under your eyes from child to girl to woman. A bundle of contradictions. A fastidious tomboy. An aesthetic glutton. What was Mitch? Quicksilver. She ran out of your hands. She was motion. Going to be a dancer. That was the only key. Could there be enough sheer mischief . . . or some dream, not known, behind those pale brown eyes? A little riddle, and as smart, he thought, as a treeful of little old owls.

None of them were stupid.

Taffy? He skipped on.

Davey, the baby. Well, hardly. Not the quick skill to use in pouring poison from one small bottleneck into another. Or in moving about, snatching the chance. Unless, of course, he had done it earlier in the day, slowly and laboriously, as clumsy as might be, unobserved and unhurried.

Duff winced again. That would be Taffy. The grave, sweet, unhurried precision of Taffy. Medicine for her dolls. Mustn't touch, that's poison. But Mommy said . . . And Brownie was mean.

No.

Davey didn't know truth from poetry. Davey couldn't, he guessed, reach the key in the stable, even standing on a box.

And if—if it had been any of these who'd used the key, Paul had covered up. And if—if it had been any of these who touched the poisoned wine bottle, had Dinny wiped it off? And . . . ? No, she couldn't have put *Eve*'s prints back on it.

Of course, Mitch, by accident, as she'd said, had wiped the other bottle. The importance of fingerprints, he thought, would be apparent to Dinny, to Paul, to

Alfie. But would the little ones have even heard of fingerprints? Surely not. Not enough to handle with gloves that guilty bottle. Or would Mitch? On the borderline of grownup knowledge.

Mary's children. All hers, as Eve had said of herself. Denis Moriarity had given them up and gone.

How far, though? *Where* was he? Mary's husband, Taffy's father, Professor Moriarity, the smell in Denmark, the joker in the woodpile, the insect in the ointment, the thorn in Duff's flesh!

After lunch, Duff went downtown.

CHAPTER 11

But, of course," said Miss Constance Avery, "what you do is get rid of the imperfect. You have to be absolutely ruthless. You can't possibly make any progress until you're convinced of that."

She sat gracefully erect in one of the two chairs on Mary's terrace that had no footrest, so that her narrow left foot in a well-cut brown and white spectator shoe rested flat on the stones and the right ankle lay gracefully across it. She wore a pale green linen dress and a short white jacket. Around her neck a yellow scarf was smartly careless.

"I don't see how you can do it," Eve Meredith blurted. "I should think you couldn't help loving them all." She had one leg wound around the other until her feet crossed each other pigeon-toed, and she huddled against the arm of her chair as if she were cold, although the late afternoon was balmy with June.

The doctor, with a footrest, lay and sipped his drink and looked up at the leaves. He seemed to be relaxing.

Duff stayed where he was a moment, in the garden door from the house, behind them. Mary, he noticed, was drawn a little away from the others, on her knees at the edge of the terrace, her fingers busy among the little plants there. She was looking down.

"Oh, no," said Constance brightly, "you soon learn to care most for the perfect puppies. After all, you must remember what you are trying to do. Once you let yourself love them just because they are alive . . ." She moved her shoulders. "Of course, it does seem cruel and harsh, but don't you see that it's really just a way of hurrying along the natural process? Sooner or later, nature eliminates the weak. Or so we hope. Very well, then. If we can understand and encourage the process, we ought to do it. Some day," she said firmly, "we will begin to apply what we have learned about animals to the breeding of humans. And then we shall speed up the progress of the world."

"You don't mean that!" said Eve explosively.

Mary looked up quickly, saw Duff, smiled and said gaily, "Hello. Come and have a drink." She waved toward the tray with earth-stained fingers. "Fix Mr. Duff a drink, Norry, please. As usual, I've got myself filthy."

Duff strolled into the group and took himself a place. The doctor said, "Say when," and Duff said, "When." Eve was looking at him with a furrowed brow as if she would like to know what he had been up to. But Miss Avery's gray gaze passed him over coolly.

The doctor climbed clumsily back into his chair. Duff settled down like a stretching cat. "What doesn't she mean?" he said lazily, prompting them to continue.

Mary was disappointed in him. Somehow, he read

that in the turning away of her face.

"I was speaking of my work with dogs," said Constance, as to a rather dull pupil. "I happen to believe rather thoroughly in the application of the principles of eugenics. I should like to see some of the things we know so well applied to the betterment of the human race."

"What race, Miss Avery?"

"All races," she snapped. "It's a great deal more simple than you think. A question of preventing the unfit from reproducing themselves." She shrugged daintily again, a tiny movement of her linen-covered shoulders.

"It is simple if you think of humans in the mass," Duff said.

"Of course."

"But the mass only exists by a great over-simplification. Once you try to saw yourself off a piece of mass with which to, let us say, experiment, you find it dissolves like mist. Or like matter, it's full of holes."

Constance bent on him an animated look. "You are sentimental," she said pityingly. "You're an individualist."

Duff said, "I'm an individual. I can't help it. Neither can you. It's our human trait and our difference."

She said angrily, "You *are* sentimental. Most people are. But I, myself, do not believe, for instance, that I have the *right* to mate myself with a blood line that would tend to degenerate the race. I think it is everyone's moral duty to consider these things."

Mary said, "Have another drink, Constance," rather dryly.

Duff said gently, "You are too sure of your facts."

148

"What do you mean?"

"I mean we do not know enough to guarantee that we could plan our own breeding better than nature does."

"Nature," said Constance scornfully. "I suppose you mean by that falling in love? That sort of thing? Don't you see it simply isn't necessary to fall in love with the wrong person?"

"Dear me," said Duff.

"You can't," said Constance with a ladylike snarl, "fall in love with people with whom you do not associate."

"But if you have, let us say, an emotional accident?" Duff could feel that there was tension on the terrace, that Eve and the doctor and Mary were disturbed, that they wished this argument would not go on. Eve twitched. Mary's hands flew among the plants with an effect of agitation. The doctor's glass sloped in his hand, and he cleared his throat twice, as if in warning.

"Then you must deplore it," said Constance airily, "and give it up. It is your duty to give it up. Furthermore, we ought to sterilize the insane, the feeble ones, the ones without the moral stamina to mate wisely or not at all. Weed them out. Get rid of them. It wouldn't take so many generations."

"How do you know?"

"Why, everybody knows . . ."

"Indeed? On what basis would you do the weeding?"

"It could be done by trained people," she snapped.

"Trained by whom?"

"By those who understand these things better than you seem to."

Eve's hands were hidden in the pockets of her skirt,

but the fingers were twisting and her eyes cast dark glances, angry looks. The doctor's face was flushed. He sat up a little straigher. He wanted to stop this and didn't know how. Mary's hands were moving more slowly. She tweaked out a tiny weed, delicately, and her fingers moulded and patted the soil. She kept her head down. Constance said, as if this were very handsome of her, "I'm sorry to seem rude, Mr. Duff, but I have no patience with your attitude."

Duff said, "I know. You believe in mass slashes, big, broad strokes, let the knife slice where it may. Whereas I believe, alas, in individual justice. Although I do not know, yet, where it can be infallibly found. But I wish it were more firmly our ideal. I wish all our prejudices, which consist of judging people in a mass, could be dissolved in the ideal of judging the individual for what he is, no matter with what handicap or so-called handicap he started."

Constance laughed. "It's rather a large handicap to start with bad blood," she jeered, "and I don't think you can call it a prejudice to wish to have nothing to do with such people."

"You must make your individual choice," Duff told her. "But I don't give you the right to make mine for me. I suspect you would breed out some things I, on the contrary, should value and wish to develop. I simply don't think"——he smiled suddenly, softening his words——"that you know enough."

Constance's lips closed in a hard line. Eve wiggled out of her chair. "Excuse me," she said hoarsely, "but I've got to go."

"Good-by, Eve." The doctor caught her hand as she was about to brush him by. She pulled it away. Her somber eyes seemed to brood on his face a moment. Then her voice went into its high gear. "Good-by, all," she said shrilly. "Thanks so much, Mary. I'll see you all again. Good-by."

Constance said, breaking the silence Eve left behind her, "Wasn't that rather rude?"

Mary got up from her knees and went quietly, without saying anything, to the house door and vanished.

The doctor looked very much distressed. He turned his eyeglasses toward Constance, on whose face the eyebrows were arched in pretty amazement. "What on earth . . . ?" she said.

"You dropped a brick," he told her, quite shortly. "I'm afraid I ought to have kicked you in the ankle."

"Well . . . really!" she said.

"I'm sorry," Duff said warmly.

"But it was simply a discussion," Constance said. "If people can't understand that things are being said quite objectively . . ."

"It isn't very pleasant . . ." Dr. Christenson stopped himself and got up. "Shall we run along, darling?"

Constance looked a little bewildered, but she got up, too.

"Mr. Duff,"—the doctor turned—"I meant to ask you before this. Look here, do you plan to stay over tonight again?" Duff let polite surprise show on his face. "I thought perhaps . . . There's a room at my house and you are very welcome to it."

Duff's eyes slid to Constance's face. It was looking rather smug now.

"I don't know that I had decided," he drawled. "I've been busy. That's very kind of you, sir."

"Then you will come?" The doctor sighed with relief and looked at Constance, too.

That one stood very straight and slender, her white coat jutting out smartly, her rosy fingers busy with the inevitable gloves.

"May I let you know?" Duff said. "It may be that I will be obliged to go into town. I'm not sure."

"Of course. Any time." The doctor began to shoulder Constance along.

Duff said smoothly, although he wanted to jab, "By the way, Miss Avery, you do use nicotine in connection with your chickens . . . do you not?"

She tilted her head. The hands stopped working on the gloves and froze in a position of attention. "Why, yes," she said.

"Then you have it on hand, of course."

"Usually," she admitted. "But as a matter of fact"—her words began to patter out in a quick rippling—"I didn't happen to have any, did I, Norris? I must remember . . ."

"You didn't happen to have any, when?" purred Duff.

"Yesterday," she said. "That is to say, Saturday. Over the week end." She smoothed the thumb of her glove. "I used all I had," she added serenely. The butter-colored head tilted again. "Did you want some, Mr. Duff? For what purpose?"

"That's what Brownie died of," growled the doctor. His eyes shot lightning.

"Oh?" said Constance. "Did she really?"

Mary met them in the hall and said good-by. Duff could hear, from where he remained, the cadences of leave-taking. He took a turn or two across the flagstones, floor-pacing in the best tradition. He bit his thumb. He went indoors after they had gone.

Mary made an effort to smile at him. "Eve's asked them to tea tomorrow," she murmured absent-mindedly. "I wonder if she'll go."

"Miss Avery?"

"Our Miss Avery!" said Mary contemptuously. Then her blue eyes clouded with anger, met his. "She annoyed me."

"I should think she would annoy nearly every one," Duff said mildly, hiding his panic, hiding his fear. "Do you know anything," he went on, "about this little plan for me? I understand I am invited to the doctor's."

Mary didn't smile. "You know you could stay here for all of me," she said soberly. "It was Constance's idea. I don't see why . . ."

"Propriety?"

"Of course." Mary's breathing was angry now. "I'd just as lief defy her and her propriety."

"But I think we won't defy her," Duff said. He wanted to add, "Don't let me do you any more harm!" He added instead, clutching at any excuse to give to Mary, "There's a chap staying with the doctor. I—er—I'd like to see a little more of him."

"Mr. O'Leary?"

"Do you know him?"

"Why, I've seen him," she said, with an odd little turn to her voice. Curiosity, perhaps. "But you *will* stay for dinner?" she added warmly.

"I'd like to."

"Good. It'll be another hour." She fluttered toward the kitchen.

"I'll go talk to Taffy, if I may," he said, smiling his

153

very best, keeping the panic down.

So he went upstairs, alone, and found Taffy sitting in a broth of toys that boiled and bubbled over the bed and onto the floor on all sides. She didn't look sick at all. She was coloring a picture. Her little fingers worked precisely. She held her tongue at the corner of her pretty mouth. She was purpling a cow.

Duff said he'd never seen a purple cow.

Taffy pointed with her crayon. "Well," she said. Her terminal l's were all o's. "There's one!" She gave out two notes of laughter. "Wouldn't it be silly if the *milk* was purple?"

"Have you got a chocolate-colored crayon?"

Taffy's face lit with delight.

Oh, Lord, none of them were stupid! These strange, big and little people. These new mixtures, reshuffled chromosomes or whatever, these individuals, different from all others.

On whose toes, cried Duff's fear to his listening anxiety, on whose toes fell the brick that Constance dropped? On Mary's? If so, then these children, who were only half Mary's, might have in their heritage what Constance called bad blood.

Duff's spirit was sick. Was this why Mary worried so? Had these six lovely children a doubt behind them, a flaw, something possibly wrong, something to be watched for, something that might come out, a reason *why* she couldn't prophesy? Could Taffy, who looked perfect, with her clear intelligence in her beautiful little body, carry, nevertheless, the seeds of madness or the seeds of crime?

Duff felt angry. It could not be so. And yet, what if it

154

were so? He felt he would rather believe MacDougal Duff was mad.

Taffy said, "Davey's getting so he doesn't go outside the lines, either. He's getting good. See what he did?"

Duff saw and admired. Was it a new coloring book?

"Pretty new," Taffy told him. "Brownie brang it to me." She looked up, a shrewd, swift look. "Brownie died, didn't she?"

"Yes," he said.

"I thought you had to be a hundred," said Taffy, back at work.

Duff's heart lightened. "Did you, Taffy? No, people sometimes don't wait that long to die."

"That's what Mommy said. Mommy said, and sometimes they're more than a hundred. Are you a hundred?"

"Not yet."

"I'm seven. Mommy's thirty-seven."

Duff swallowed. He could say now, *if* he could, "Taffy, did you put anything in a wine bottle yesterday? Before you got sick? Remember?" But the trouble was that he couldn't. He could not ask her. He told himself, hastily, that he must not put such a nasty thought into her little mind, lest she be innocent. He told himself she'd had a fever. She wouldn't remember. Would never remember. He looked down at the pretty little paw guiding the crayon so carefully within the lines, and he groaned.

"Have you got a headache?" said Taffy.

"Maybe a little one." He smiled at her. He put a finger on her smooth cheek, as one would pet a kitten.

"When's your birthday?" said MacDougal Duff with stiff, cowardly lips.

Taffy immediately invited him to her birthday. It was, she explained, customary to bring a present. "But you don't *haf* to." Then she invited him to read her a story.

So Duff sat back against the headboard and read aloud the trials and tribulations and triumphs of one Cinderella, with the little creature beside him listening, close against him, just as if the plot hadn't been much fresher to him than it was to her.

Mary found them, like that, when she brought a tray for Taffy and told Duff his dinner was ready.

Duff went downstairs beside her, walking on clouds with a pink sunset in his head. He did not feel like deducing anything.

CHAPTER 12

Dr. Norris Christenson lived in a small detached house, one wing of which was his office. The room that served him for both living and dining quarters was by no means as cool and airy as Mary's house, this warm June evening. Duff came in at about nine o'clock. Mr. Oliver O'Leary was ensconced there, in a leather chair beside the window. He was reading a large and unfrivolous-looking book and wore horn-rimmed glasses which he seemed to need for this purpose. From time to time he shifted on the leather, with the faintest of ripping sounds, as if he were sticking to it and moved to unstick himself.

The doctor greeted Duff with great cordiality and offered him cool alcoholic refreshment. He acted like a man who lived well in a comfortable, not elegant, middle-class kind of way. His house had no decorative coherence. It was a bachelor's house, and basically conventional. The doctor settled with his guest across the room from O'Leary, who paid them no mind, but went on reading his book.

The doctor searched Duff's long, melancholy face and began to speak lightly of the weather and one thing and another of equal unimportance.

Duff was sunk. Sunk in the chair, sunk in thought, sunk in spirits. The dread was back and the worry, and the fear that he was doing wrong. "Your county medical examiner is a jolly fellow," he said at last.

Dr. Christenson smiled and fingered his mustache.

"Very jolly," Duff repeated, "and gay, in that blunt manly manner. Oh, I talked with him this afternoon."

"Oh, you did?"

"He as much as told me, in his merry way,"—Duff was seldom sarcastic; this was a bad sign—"that if I hadn't come around and poked my nose into this business . . . my unfortunately too celebrated nose . . . he would have blithely assumed accidental death. He says he's afraid . . . afraid," Duff repeated with bitterness, "that he would have thought it absurd to suppose Mrs. Moriarity or any of her family or friends, either, would have gone to work and poisoned a guest so blatantly. Blatantly, he says."

The doctor moistened his lips. "That's too bad. Too bad. I'm sorry to hear that."

"I did my best to explain how I stumbled into the thing. I tried to explain that I had no more reason to think this was murder than he had. But he continues to believe, and nudge me in the ribs about it, that I am withholding and concealing some brilliant observation or other. Damn it all!" Duff said, "shall I go back to New York? And stay there?"

"I don't know," the doctor said uneasily. "What do you think?"

158

"I think that I shall have to solve this case whether I like it or not."

"Of course," the doctor said, "that would be . . . if you could . . ."

"If I can find a solution that satisfies," Duff muttered.

The doctor didn't answer. He nodded, a bit nervously. His glance flicked over toward O'Leary under his lamp, though Duff had been speaking in low tones. Duff shrugged.

"Shall we go into my office?" the doctor suggested.

"Not necessary," Duff murmured. He was not going to commit himself to a frank conspiracy with this man. Not tonight. Let it be understood, if it were understood, without any more words on the subject. Bad enough to conspire with himself.

"Have you seen the toxicologist's report?" he asked, more easily.

"Yes, yes. Doesn't tell us much. Can't really tell how much she actually got, you know. Have to guess what she got rid of and so forth and so forth."

"At least it tells us that both the wine and the body held more poison than could have been in the solution Paul was using on the roses."

"I never thought he had anything to do with it."

Duff agreed. "He couldn't have dealt in such strong poison from so large a container. That's what it comes down to. Not unless he had nearly a pint of the 40 per cent solution. Those little bottles hold what? An ounce? No, Paul couldn't have done it, for these and other reasons."

"Nor would have," the doctor insisted.

"We have to do a little better than 'wouldn't have.' It's better to know that the sprayer won't suck on a mere ounce. And other things of that sort. Evidence. Fact."

The doctor frowned and bit off a piece of his little fingernail. "You say Dr. Surf might have been satisfied that it was accidental?"

"They have a half-baked theory. They imagine that the bottle of wine standing open in Mrs. Meredith's house for the best part of a week may have accidentally got contaminated. They can't prove that, of course, but they seem willing to believe it, just the same. Of course, now, to believe it they are going to have to believe that Mary is lying when she says she drank the wine from her tray. And that Mitch is lying when she says she did not change the position of those damned wine bottles. They're bound to wonder why people take the trouble to lie."

The doctor looked bewildered, and Duff explained, carefully, how matters stood.

"Of course"—the doctor cleared his throat —"there's another—er—possible . . ."

"Go on."

"Suppose Dinny is mistaken about which bottle she used to pour the wine for her mother? That would explain her—er—fingerprints . . ."

"She poured it from the one on the table, you mean? Therefore, the bottles *weren't* switched? The poison was put in just after Dinny left?"

"No, no. I mean, of course the bottles were switched. But the wine in the pantry was—er —poisoned, let us say, at Eve's."

"I see what you're after," said Duff. "You're trying to let Mary tell the truth and still have the wine poisoned at Eve's by accident. But why would Dinny make such an odd mistake as that? Or do you mean *she* lied? I don't see why. Do you?"

"No," the doctor said, "no, still . . . children."

Duff looked a bit contemptuous. "Oh, I grant you if we begin to go into the possibility of lying, we run into all sorts of thoughts. Dinny lied and touched both bottles. Paul lied by covering up someone's fingerprints on that little bottle of poison that was found in the stable."

"But—"

"Why? Yes, there again, I don't see why. How would he know it was necessary or desirable?"

"He was in the stable afterward."

"After she died?"

"Yes, after she died." The doctor squirmed and Duff frowned.

"One thing I do see," said Duff: "something is wrong with Alfie's testimony."

"What's that?"

"Alfie claims to have been sent, or at least to have gone, out to the back porch, just outside the dining room. He claims that no one entered the dining room at all while he was there. Now, he was there between the time Brownie was dying, and the time, or close to the time, the police came."

"He may be right."

"Yes," said Duff thoughtfully, "he may. But Dinny says the toaster was on when she and the small ones left the room. The police say it was off when they entered. Who turned it off, doctor? Someone did. Therefore, it seems to me, someone went into the dining room and did so. Who? And when?"

The doctor lifted his holder gracefully. "Dinny may

be mistaken. Maybe one of them turned it off so automatically that it—er—"

"Didn't register?" Duff stroked his long chin. "That's possible. Plenty of false evidence is given in this world in all sincerity. Also, I can see a tiny gap." He hesitated. "Of course, I've been wondering if someone hasn't been hiding in that house."

"Hiding!" The doctor was confounded, astonished. He sat up so fast he spilled some of his Tom Collins.

"There have been slight indications," Duff said wryly. He got a piece of paper out of his pocket. "Ever see that face?"

The doctor took it, and as he held it, it shook. He seemed unable, for a moment, to speak. He made a negative sign with his head.

"It's the picture of a man who has a reason to hide, and who must, in fact, be hiding somewhere."

"Olaf Severson, wanted . . ." the doctor read. He turned the paper over, popped his eyes out at Duff in bewilderment.

"Oh, I see things!" said Duff, snatching it back. "I hear things! I have hallucinations, maybe. Fantastic ideas roam around in the great emptiness of my head." He got up. He was an angry man, angry with himself. "I don't seem to see any way to get hold of this problem," he confessed bitterly. "So far, I have done nothing but sit around and listen and watch and make up fantasies. I have taken no steps. No steps occur to me to be taken. I am in a state. I worry about ghosts." He put his elbow on the mantel and leaned his head on his hand.

The doctor murmured sympathy. Across the room, Mr. O'Leary had pricked up his ears.

"What terrifies me," said Duff, "is the simplicity, the undetectable nonchalance, the perfect cold-bloodedness of this crime, if it is a crime. Someone puts poison in a bottle of wine. Not another thing does he do. Thinks no more about it. Simply maintains that he did not. Suppose there are no nerves involved. Suppose . . ."

"I see what you mean," said Mr. O'Leary crisply. "A childlike quality. Yes."

Duff stared at him. He vaguely considered the American idiom, 'I see what you mean' and the rather stagey effect of that British intonation.

"You must give it over to your subconscious," said Mr. O'Leary emphatically.

"My subconscious," said Duff without smiling, "is at the moment an incompetent mess. I'd hate to rely on it." He turned his back. "Look here, doctor, one thing you can tell me. What brick did Miss Avery drop this afternoon?"

"Brick?"

"Surely you remember."

"Oh. She—er—when you and she got into an argument? Connie rides her hobby horse a little hard."

Duff's eye gleamed. "Is Eve Meredith, perhaps, on the verge of insanity?"

"Insanity!" The doctor's eyes rolled. "Good heavens, I shouldn't say so. High-strung Eve is, always has been. But she's devoted to her son, of course. And in a bad state of anxiety right now. War nerves, one might say. Well accounted for in her case. I mean to say, naturally she's anxious. Who isn't? And being a very nervous woman, she is much affected. But insane? No."

Duff sat down again. "I think," he said wearily, "you had better tell me more about Denis Moriarity. Was *he* insane? Or in any way a little off?"

"Dear me," said the doctor. "Dear me. Why, not that I ever knew. Of course, I never knew him too well. But there was no hint of such a thing. No hint at all. I do think you must be . . . confused."

Duff caught the impression of great care. The doctor was walking softly, watching his own words, pussy-footing.

O'Leary said, "There is a great deal of loose talk about insanity." His mouth snapped shut again.

"Are you a psychiatrist, among other things, Doctor?" Duff wondered.

"No, no, not at all. I mean to say, no more than any doctor has to be. But I assure you, there is no insanity involved here. That I know of."

"What was the dropped brick, then?" Duff persisted.

"Oh, class," the doctor said. "Class consciousness. Connie . . . I'm afraid . . ."

"Whose class? Was Moriarity a social error?"

"No, no. But I believe Eve's people were . . . from humble sources."

Again Duff sensed the care, the caution, the pussy-foot.

"I don't know, of course," the doctor said. "All that I meant this afternoon . . . I felt that Connie was being rather high and mighty. I know Mary was annoyed. Connie gets carried away, sounds much more —er—rude and intolerant, believe me, than she means to be. She's so direct, you know, so—"

"Tell me," Duff broke in, "why did Moriarity get out? Why leave that family? What happened?"

"To the marriage, you mean?"

"Yes, to the marriage."

"Why," the doctor spread his fingers, "I can't tell you exactly. My impression, if you are interested in that?"

"I am."

"My impression was that their lives diverged. Mary, after all, was pretty much absorbed out here with all those children, her house, domestic life. Whereas Denis, of course, traveled in theatrical circles, met people who were not in the least domestic, people who had other ideas."

Duff looked down at his shoes. "Was there what is known as another woman?"

"Oh, I'm afraid so," the doctor said sadly.

"Who?"

"Don't know. Understand, I don't even know that there was. I suspect. It seems likely." The doctor wiped his face.

"I'm sorry," said Duff. "This hurts me as much as it does you, you know. This kind of question."

"What I don't understand is why you are so much concerned, if that is the right word, with Moriarity." The doctor was pussy-footing again. "Really, I don't see what he has or could have to do with this . . . this poison business."

"Oh, neither do I," Duff said. "Neither do I, I assure you. I don't really see anything at all." His despair came over him again and his great dissatisfaction with himself. "Something seems to have gone wrong with my faculties. I haven't asked the right questions," he said heavily. "I don't analyze. I drift. I don't follow a direct line. I veer. I wander. I am not organized. I am not logical. One must, at least, begin with logic. And I haven't begun at all. I am making no real investigation whatsoever. I am batted around by worries. I do not think. And even my intuition, which sometimes saves me, has gone to hell."

"Go to bed," the doctor said softly. "You need rest. Forget about it, if you can. Believe me, Mr. Duff, that is good advice. Things may not be so confusing, or so bad, in the morning."

"Better take his advice," said O'Leary in his crisp sudden way. "He is a very wise man, Mr.—er—Duff."

"Very well. I will go to bed." Duff got up. Added to the rest, now, was shame for having confessed before them. Duff's feeling of personal disintegration was intolerably painful. Into his head had run the thought that Mary must have been relieved to get him away from the house. Of course, if Moriarity was there, she would need to talk to him. She would not have wanted Duff to know how relieved she was. She would have acted as she had acted.

He bit hard on nothing, pressing his teeth tight.

"Remember your dreams," said O'Leary, as one who gives a hot tip or betrays a secret process. "Try to remember what you dream."

The doctor took Duff off to his room, and Mr. O'Leary, with a sad knowing little smile on his lips, went back to his reading.

Dr. Christenson's housekeeper was a colored woman of great size who seemed to consider breakfast for three men a nine-egg affair. Mr. O'Leary was there, spruce and trim, resisting her coaxing. The doctor was there, too, not quite so spruce, looking a bit rumpled and heavy-eyed, as Duff came down.

O'Leary put cream in his coffee, measuring it carefully on his spoon. "Did you write it down?" he demanded brightly. Duff looked at him. "Your dream, of course."

"No, but I dreamed. I remember."

"Dreams are very interesting," said the little man in his clipped accent. "Don't you think so? Clues, really."

"Clues?"

"To oneself. Tell the doctor."

"Does the doctor interpret dreams?"

The doctor nibbled bacon. "O'Leary thinks I can," he said, "but I'm a pure amateur."

"I have put myself in Dr. Christenson's hands this summer," said O'Leary, "with the greatest confidence."

Duff sighed. He did not feel rested. The sense of inner confusion still pained and distressed him. "What do you make of this, then?" he asked. "I was in a hall . . ."

O'Leary put down his fork and bent toward him to listen. The doctor went on with his bacon and only occasionally flashed his eye over the coffee cup in Duff's direction.

". . . an auditorium or theater in which there was a large audience of people gathered. I was among them. Someone, a man, I think . . . a person . . . was on the stage talking. It may have been a lecture. I don't remember what he said. But I was very uncomfortable and uneasy because the spotlight, if that's what it was . . . or in some way, some kind of light . . . was focused on me. I kept squirming away from it, but it stayed on me. I didn't like it.

"The dream melted and dissolved—you know how dreams do—and suddenly I was on the stage myself, or rather backstage, and I seemed to be trying very hard to get this speaker, the one who had been talking, into a small place like a dressing room and get the door shut before they came."

"Who?"

"The audience. The people seemed to be surging up at me over the footlights. There was danger in that. I had to get the door shut. I strained at it in that futile way . . ."

"Frustration," murmured O'Leary. "Yes . . ."

"But," said Duff, "I did get it shut in time. I was not frustrated. I managed it. Then there was another dissolve, and I was on the stage alone with a broad beam of light as if from a movie projector, leading from where I was to the balcony. In the balcony"—he hesitated—"there was a very lovely lady. I began to walk up the beam of light, and it held me. I daresay," he said, pulling his mouth down at all this nonsense, "I was about halfway there, walking on air, of course, when I woke up."

"Ah!" breathed Mr. O'Leary, and he turned bright, interested eyes on the doctor.

"Well, obviously," said the doctor, "you were afraid of something."

Duff nodded. He plunged into his grapefruit.

"Probably the spotlight on you meant that the speaker was talking about you. So you had to —er—shut him up. You see?"

"Of course!" O'Leary crowed. "That's very interesting. Translation of the phrase 'shut him up' into closing the door. Shutting him up literally. Eh, doctor?"

"I think so," said the doctor. He seemed to enjoy this. "Then, having conquered that which you feared, you—er—well, next came your reward. The beautiful lady, eh? That's a success dream, Mr. Duff."

"Meaning?"

The doctor shrugged. "I don't really know," he said. "I only guess at these things. You mustn't take me seriously. I think perhaps it means effort, determination, resolve. You are afraid of something, but you are going to fight it. Eh?"

"Thank you," said Duff thoughtfully.

"Are you going to the funeral?"

"No. I think not."

Mr. O'Leary got up from the table very abruptly. His head back, chin in, he looked past his nose at the doctor with reproach. In fact, he looked as if he were going to cry. "I shall walk ten miles," he said, "that is, if I *can*, now. Until lunch, then."

"I'm sorry," said the doctor. "Yes, ten miles this morning. But take them easy. You can do it."

When O'Leary had gone, the doctor began to explain that he ought not to have mentioned a funeral before O'Leary, whose nerves were shaken by all such words. Duff only half listened.

"Just one more question," he broke in. "I see I must ask you." The doctor's hand stopped buttering toast. "Because, of course, you know what we are both afraid of."

The doctor blinked.

"Tell me," said Duff solemnly, his heart contracting,

"for any reason, are you *sure?*"

"Sure?"

"Yes. Have you a reason I know nothing about for thinking Taffy . . . guilty?"

The doctor put down his knife and smoothed his mustache with a thoughtful finger. "No," he said. "Of course not."

Oh, God, thought Duff, don't *handle* me! Don't treat me like a patient! He said aloud, "You know of nothing, beyond what I know?"

"No, nothing," said the doctor. "I am *not* sure. It's just . . ." He spread out his hands. His eyes looked miserable and watchful behind the lenses.

"Is Mary going to the funeral?"

"Yes, I think she is going with the Lomaxes. Friends."

"I see. I had better not go."

"Perhaps it's better if you don't. What will you do?"

"I'm going to lay a ghost," Duff said grimly, "if I can."

"What ghost? What do you mean? You said something about a ghost last night, too. I don't . . ."

"Neither do I understand," said Duff, "but I am a haunted man, doctor. And before I can get anywhere at all in this thing, I've got to lay a ghost."

The doctor looked helpless and let him go.

CHAPTER 13

Duff drove his car down Mary's street; and there, coming out of her front door at nine-thirty in the morning, bold as brass, was none other than Mr. Haggerty.

Duff slid slyly to the curb, waited, and as his victim came jauntily to the sidewalk, turning his toes out, sniffing the morning, Duff pounced.

"Where have you been?"

Haggerty jumped and peered dramatically through the car window. "Ah, there, Mr. Duff. Good morning. Good morning."

"Where have you been?" said Duff again. "I've missed you."

"I've been"—Haggerty's eyes rolled as if he skirted on a secret matter—"away."

"Away?" Duff drawled.

"Yes, away."

Vaudeville, thought Duff. "Not keeping an eye on

the premises last night, then?" he challenged. "Not lurking?"

"No. Er . . . no." Haggerty denied it judiciously. His fingers went to his coat pocket and pulled out the notebook. "Would you care to tell me what happened?" he inquired politely.

"Nothing happened, as far as I know," snapped Duff.

"Perhaps I—er—misunderstood."

They eyed each other.

"By the way," said Haggerty, "a Mr. Maguire was on the telephone, within the moment. I happened to take the call." Duff's eyes glittered. "He refused, however, to give me any—er—dope," said Haggerty, "although I explained to him that you and I had reached an understanding."

Duff said nothing at all. His silence was enough comment.

"Mr. Maguire went on to say," Haggerty went on with a little less aplomb, "he had nothing that seems too terribly important."

"Too terribly?"

"Sorry. My adverbs." Haggerty bowed an apology. "He said, 'Tell the boss I'll give him what I got later. It can wait.' " The mimicry wasn't bad. But Haggerty dropped it quickly and went back to his own peculiar style. "He further said that he cannot be reached for an hour or two because he is going—er—away."

"Thank you so much," said MacDougal Duff.

"Oh, don't mention it. Of course, if you would care to know where he is going and what he will find out when he gets there . . ."

"Naturally, I'd be pleased," Duff responded. This

172

phony courtesy was catching.

"Since I have already been there . . ."

"Been where?"

Haggerty looked hurt. "This is a guess, of course," he said.

"Oh, go ahead, guess. Pray do."

"Very well."

Duff thought to himself that "Very well" was a phrase used only in moments of self-conscious stuffiness. Haggerty, however, seemed to think it was a normal equivalent of "O.K." The man talked as if his part had been written by a bad playwright, and Duff had caught the thing from him. This whole dialogue was preposterous.

"I believe," said Haggerty, "that in an hour or two your Mr. Maguire will be making inquiries at the Boone Home for the Mentally Ill in Haytonville."

"Indeed?"

"Inquiries about Mrs. Eve Norden Meredith's mother's sister." Haggerty lowered his lids modestly.

"Who is, I presume, an inmate there?"

"Who was. Deceased, 1940."

"Insane?"

"Oh, yes, indeedy," said Haggerty.

Duff leaned back. "Now, I wonder why this interests you and Mr. Maguire."

"It interests us," intoned Haggerty, "because Miss Emily Brown seems to have stumbled upon what was a family—er—skeleton." One would think he had invented the phrase at the spur of the moment.

"Oh, let me guess," said Duff. "So she told Eve's husband and frightened him away."

"Yes, she told Eve's husband. The baby, Ralph, was

173

very small. The husband did go away. He was a matter-of-fact man, himself. He was practical. He didn't fancy the connection. He seems to have believed himself the victim of fraud and deception, the injured party."

"And where is he now, we wonder."

To Duff's surprise, Haggerty answered. "In Washington, I believe."

Duff thumped the upholstery of his car with his fist. "In Washington? Alive? Real, eh? Located and found to be himself and nobody else?"

"But . . . aren't we all?" said Haggerty with terrific delicacy.

Duff looked coldly at him. "I must say this comes in very pat."

Haggerty ducked the implied accusation. "Why, thank you," he said gracefully.

"Can you tell me out of your omniscience, Mr. Haggerty, where Professor Moriarity is now?"

Haggerty smiled a bright mechanical smile as one whose boss has made a not very funny joke. "As a matter of fact, I did happen to ask a friend of mine in a casting agency. It seems Moriarity—Professor's very good, sir, ha ha—Moriarity has changed his name again."

"His habit."

"You knew that? Yes, a habit of his. However, this time he seems to have dropped completely out of sight. At least, so far as my friend knows."

"Is *he* crazy?"

"Who?"

"Moriarity?"

"Crazy?"

"You do know what I mean?"

174

Haggerty took out the notebook and made a note of it. Afterwards, he said, "I do not know, sir. He may be. The rumor is that he's involved with a wealthy woman."

"Or not so crazy," snapped Duff. He unlatched the car door. "Get in and sit down," he said briskly.

It seemed to be part of Haggerty's code to obey such a sudden instruction without curiosity. He got in and sat down. Duff said, "Identify yourself, please."

Haggerty got out a leather and celluloid case and displayed a driver's license issued to one Francis Xavier Haggerty, male, white, height 5ft. 11in., col. of hair brown, col. of eyes brown, age twenty-eight.

"You don't look it," Duff said.

"Pardon?"

"Age twenty-eight."

"Why, thank you," said Francis Xavier. "Social Security, sir?"

"Never mind."

"Draft number?" Haggerty said a little anxiously, "I presume you mean I appear older?"

Duff said, indifferently, "Never mind. I see you have papers."

Haggerty said, "Who do you think I am!"

"I think you're an odd duck, whoever you are, Mr. Haggerty. Pray pay no attention to my rude and suspicious nature. And do tell me, is Mrs. Moriarity at home this morning?"

"No, not at the moment. She left the house half an hour ago. For the funeral, I understood."

"But you saw her this morning?"

"Certainly. For a moment or two."

"What have you been doing since she left?"

"Chatting with the children," said Haggerty, brushing his lapels as if he had suddenly discovered dust on them.

"And who do you think did it, Mr. Haggerty?"

"I should like to ask you that question, sir. In fact, it is time, is it not, that I asked a question or two and you did the answering? According to compact."

"According to mythical compact, yes, to be sure." Duff put his neck on the back of the seat and looked at the flannelly gray inside of the car's top. "I can't answer any questions because I don't know any answers. All I have, my dear Haggerty, is perhaps a small nebulous nudge from the subconscious." Duff could be cryptic and romantic, too. "Let us say, a little hovering of the wing of truth, a feather touch . . ."

"A hunch!" breathed Haggerty in an awed whisper.

Duff controlled his smile. "Do you believe in hunches?" he crooned. "Tip-offs from the subconscious, aren't they? Clues, as our friend O'Leary puts it. Do you know O'Leary? No? Well, let me tell you my dream, Mr. Haggerty"—Duff slid farther down in the seat and let his voice murmur—"for I have been dreaming. I was in a hall . . ."

He told his dream all the way through, and Haggerty made a silent audience. "Well?" said Duff when he had finished.

Mr. Haggerty frowned. For a moment, Duff thought he wasn't going to play any more. He did stretch a leg and feel of it as if to see whether it had been pulled. "What does it mean?" Duff insisted.

"I should say it meant you were ambitious," intoned Haggerty.

"Brutus says Caesar was ambitious."

176

"Eh?"

"Go on."

"Ambitious to do your job, of course. Anxious. The spotlight is your responsibility. And it would seem"—that ponderous delicacy came in again—"you wish to catch your man. Was the lecturer a man?"

"I'm not sure," said Duff cautiously.

"In any case, you caught him."

"And the people surging over the footlights?"

"That means you want to catch himself yourself, alone, first, before they do," said Haggerty rapidly.

"I see. I see."

"As for the end of your dream, when you walked on light, well, might not the light be inspiration? Seeing the light, sir? Leading you to a woman? Leading you—to a woman!" he repeated in his awed romantic way.

Duff laughed. "I find that dream more and more fascinating," he said carelessly. "Thanks for your comment. And for your information, of course."

Haggerty didn't want to be dismissed. He put on a hurt look and sat still. But Duff reached across and unlatched the door. "I'll—er—see you later," he said, making the phrase sound heavy with hint and mystery. Therefore, as he had judged, Haggerty accepted it. He got out and bowed Duff out.

"How much later, do you think?" he asked.

"Oh, five-ish," Duff waved a hand. Haggerty saluted and went off up the street, jauntily, turning out his toes.

Dinny was on the phone, ordering groceries from a scribbled list. Taffy was up and out, sitting in the sun on the terrace with Davey and Mitch and seven stuffed toy animals. The boys were taking a bicycle apart, in the stable. Duff looked in and found them smudged and absorbed, but they followed him back toward the house as if he were bound to be more interesting than Alfie's coaster brake.

Dinny joined them on the back porch. Duff was peering through the curtained French doors. The eastern sun at the side window made the interior of the dining room perfectly visible. Yet late in the day or in the rain, he realized, this would not be true.

Alfie said he hadn't tried to look in, anyhow.

Duff sat on the porch rail. He took a notion. He followed the impulse to tell them his dream.

"Something you et," said Alfie at the end. "What'd you have? Cheese?"

"No cheese."

"Sauerkraut?"

"No sauerkraut."

"Gosh," said Alfie, "I had a nightmare once on top of sauerkraut, boy!"

"Shaddup," said Paul.

"What do you suppose it means?" Duff asked them again.

"Doesn't have to mean anything, does it?" said Paul kicking at the floor.

Dinny said, "I don't see any sense to it."

"None at all? What was I trying to do? Why?"

"Well," she said, "it looks as if you were trying to protect that speaker or whoever it was. Trying to keep him safe from the crowd." Duff nodded. "Well, you did it. That's all," she said.

"And the rest?"

"Oh, that's your sex life," said Dinny blandly. Then

178

she retreated to the fake fumbling with words she put on for the benefit of most of her elders. "I mean, isn't that what dreams are supposed to be? I mean, aren't they? You know, Freud? I mean, I don't know . . ."

Paul looked up from his feet. "Yeah, but I don't see why locking up a man doesn't go with the idea that you are a detective. I mean, it might. You're supposed to get people into jail, aren't you?"

"That's an idea," murmured Duff. "Yes, I suppose I am."

"And the beautiful dame," said Paul, "is just a beautiful dame, maybe you're in love with. Or maybe it's your mother or somebody."

The sunny morning tipped and shimmered and righted itself. Duff got off the railing, breathing hard. "Look here," he commanded them. He stood so tall and looked so suddenly alert and determined that they shrank away and their three frightened faces turned up at him, wide and white of eye. "Get me a picture of your father!" roared MacDougal Duff, at least as close to a roar as ever his gentleness could come.

"A p-picture of Dad?"

"If you please!"

"But . . ." Dinny looked helpless.

"Gee," said Alfie, "I dunno where there *is* any."

"Do *you?*"

"No," said Paul. "We just haven't got one, unless Mother knows."

"Anything will do. A snap. A sketch."

They were dumb. They shook their heads.

"I can search the house," he threatened.

"O.K. We'll help you," said Alfie cordially, but the other two remained as if numbed with surprise.

179

Somebody burst out of the back door and ran down the drive. There was a flash of faded blue as somebody ran into the stable. Duff was off the porch and at the stable door quicker than the kids behind him. When those three saw that it was their mother in her blue jeans and working shirt, with her face grim, they surged past him and stood around her like a guard.

Mary snatched at a hoe. In spite of her expression, she looked very young. Her hair was tousled. The blue pants were old and worn and fit her well. She had on flat round-toed brown shoes, scuffed like a boy's. She looked, Duff thought, with a queer shamed pang, cute.

"What's the matter?"

"Mom?"

"Did anything happen?"

"Just funerals," she said. "Don't mind me. I'm going out and dig"—she caught her breath like a sob—"in the sun. I want to get the taste of it out of my mouth."

The kids faded away. They seemed to understand immediately, and they seemed relieved, as if this were a familiar reaction once they understood what she was reacting to. Mary flashed a blue eye after them, shoved open a side door with a bang, and went out into the garden, holding her hoe like a spear.

Duff followed after. He stood in the sun and watched her as she attacked the ground among the cabbages. Mary pushed the hoe back and forth in vigorous rhythm that slowly lost haste and steam. The scuffle hoe cut under the weeds and they fell. The sun beat down. Silence surrounded them, through which the hoe crunched pleasantly. The earth turned a deeper brown where she worked, and the garden smells arose, the earthy perfume of peace.

180

MacDougal Duff in his city clothes might have been a scarecrow had the little breeze been able to swing his sleeves. It touched his hair.

"I'm such a fool," sighed Mary at last, "to hate it so much."

"I'm sure it was hateful," he said. "Mary . . ."

She leaned on her hoe. By now her face had color and some dirt on it. Her eyes were so blue and so candid, Duff held his breath.

"I had to get where things were living and growing," she told him. "I'm ashamed to have been in such a silly hurry. But when they bury me, I hope it's in topsoil. Where there's life. Even worms are life." Her mouth quivered. "There's only such a thin shell of life around the earth, a spade deep. Not much deeper."

"But a fine thing," he said, "as far as it goes."

She squinted an eye up toward the sun and then down at the cabbages. "Yes." They smiled at each other.

"I want a picture of your husband," Duff told her, as if he were taking up a train of thought they'd left off together.

In a queerly companionable way, she let the assumption stand. She showed no particular surprise or curiosity either. "I don't think I've got one," she said calmly.

For Duff, the peace was torn. "Why not?" he demanded.

Mary shrugged. She began to push the hoe. "Why don't you go ask Eve if she has one?" she suggested over her shoulder. "She's a one for albums and all that. She really might . . ."

"Very well. I will."

Very well! Duff marched off through the cabbages. He felt stiff and angry. He was under a compulsion to be rude. He kept his eyes strictly ahead, but movement in the lane, outside the garden, caught them.

He turned and walked to the fence and peered through some vines. He sang out, "Wait a minute! I say, Mr. O'Leary!"

Mr. O'Leary's strutting trot faltered. He turned his head anxiously and looked all around and then up, too, as if there might be angels. Duff's long face came through the leaves, and Mr. O'Leary jumped in his tracks like a startled rabbit.

"What are you doing here?" said Duff sternly.

"Where?" said O'Leary furiously. He put trembling fingers to his temples. "What am I doing where? What do you mean?" He stamped his foot like a child. *"Where am I?"* he screeched. Then he fumbled for the thing that looked like a watch. "Four and two-tenths miles," he read. "And what, may I ask, is that to you, sir?"

"To you it's four and two-tenths miles? That's all?"

"What's that?"

"Just your walk?"

"Naturally." O'Leary danced with rage. "I walk by doctor's orders. As you ought to know. You . . ."

"And how do you decide where to go?"

"I don't! I . . . damn it all, sir, I don't *care* where I go!"

"This is a coincidence?" Duff, with vine leaves in his hair, felt himself leering.

"What, sir! Look here, I have nearly six miles before lunch . . ."

Duff looked into his blue-gray eyes, swimming in

182

liquid outrage. "March on." He put his hand over the fence as if he held an apology in the palm of it. "I'm very sorry."

Mr. O'Leary seared the hand with a blistering glare and marched on.

Duff turned back along the path to a gap between some berry bushes, toward the lawn. Mary was slowly pushing her hoe back and forth among the silver cabbages.

Duff, although he knew now what ailed him and why he was haunted and by what, didn't look at her. It gave him bitter pleasure not to. He did wave at the children on the terrace. Then he turned off around the pool to where the white gate led to Eve's.

Behaving like a fool kid, roiled inside, sulky outside, jumping to the most absurd conclusions, nevertheless, he was bitterly happy and cherished his pain. He was in love. At his age. In love with Mary Moriarity, six children and all. He was . . . damn it . . . jealous.

He must lay the mocking ghost of Professor Moriarity.

CHAPTER 14

Beyond tbe gate, Duff crossed Eve's garden on a path to a side door. Her house was about the vintage of Mary's, although smaller. The garden was smaller, too. Duff felt sure, although he knew nothing at all about it, that it was not half so fine.

He rapped, there being no bell here. Eve was at home. Her face, reminding him again of the skull beneath it, appeared in the window, and she let him in with exclamations of welcome. Her house was full of old things, shabby things, not fine. But it was neat and nearly cozy. Eve herself, at home, was not quite so unraveled. She said she was just about to sit down to lunch and wouldn't he have some, although it was nothing much.

"Please go ahead and eat yours, Mrs. Meredith. I won't disturb you. Mrs. Moriarity sent me over to ask if you have a picture of her husband, a snap, anything. I wanted to see one."

"A picture of Denis? Why, I don't know. I did

have." Eve led him into a front sitting room. She pulled an album out from a low shelf under a little table, blew on it for dust. "I have a lot of old pictures in here. Maybe you can find one, but I don't remember exactly . . ."

"Let me look," he said quickly. "And you go back to your lunch, please."

"Well . . ."

"I see you have captions. Why, this is wonderful. I'll just sit here, if I may." Duff established himself in a chair with the album on his knees and tried to look permanent. She seemed to be standing on one foot and not sure where to plant the other.

"Mrs. Meredith, if you let me keep you I shall be offended."

"Well . . . if you're sure . . . if you don't mind . . ." He shoveled her out with more protestations, and at last she withdrew, reluctant and uncertain, looking back.

Duff opened the album. It was an old album. The photographs were held by fancy little black cut-out corners. Three or four snaps to a page, arranged in a variety of geometric designs. Under each, in white ink on the black pages, Eve had written in a round hand some comment, often identifying but sometimes merely witty. The wit was rather pathetic. "Aren't I cute?" said one.

It was Eve's own album, arranged by her, although it began earlier than herself. She soon appeared, however, in ruffles, in gingham, in high laced shoes and a middy blouse.

Duff turned the pages rapidly.

The room was still. He felt hidden, here in this strange house with its past on his knee, and some of

Mary's past, too, and perhaps a part of her future. A picture caught his eye, and he slipped his finger in the place. Not now. Later. Now he was looking for one face only, the face of Moriarity.

The room was warm. Duff felt a dew on his brow.

"Ah!"

He came to a page with three square snapshots arranged symmetrically with the place where a fourth had been. Under the square in the upper right position the white scrawl read *Mr. and Mrs. Moriarity!* The exclamation point was Eve's.

Yes—Duff's eyes lingered to make sure—it was certainly Mary, younger, but Mary herself. And the man beside her, in whose arm she had thrust her own, looked straight out of the photograph.

Duff sat entranced.

In a moment he shifted his body, crossed his leg.

He wanted to laugh.

The shock was good. His whole body tingled. A mist seemed to roll off his brain. "But I should have known," he said out loud. "Of course." He stretched out his legs, then, and slid down a little. He relaxed.

So.

Well, then . . .

He looked back at the page. At upper left the caption said *The house next door.* Duff studied that picture. It was the Moriarity house. His eye followed every line. Taken from this side. Yes. But no terrace, no roses, no vine, no dainty little tree, there at the corner. Stark and ugly it had looked in those days, when Mary's skirts were short and her hair cut like a boy's and her belt down on her hips. When? The twenties, he guessed.

Now, today, the old house dreamed in the luxury of its June garden, and it had an air. Then it had been untouched by Mary's loving skill, and it was grim. Duff was impressed. "She's wonderful!" he thought, and a part of his mind smiled at the antics of the rest. But he had it clear, now. He could make his discounts, and he could think.

He looked at the third picture. It showed him four young women in the garb of a little earlier day, who stood linked in a row in front of a porch railing. They were, of course, all laughing gaily. The caption, *Four little girls from school!* Duff examined the faces. At the left, the tallest wore a face he couldn't recognize. Next came Brownie. Big-bosomed, even then. And horsy of face. Very jolly she looked. Very bold and sure of herself. Next Mary again, smiling with some restraint, looking dainty, in a different dress and wearing her hair a little longer. That was Eve, of course, on the end. A very pretty Eve, too. Rounder and softer of cheek and body. A happy young Eve who may have been, probably was, carrying a child. That dress looked suspicious with its ties and bows. Ralph was nineteen, she'd said. Duff subtracted rapidly.

Under the place where a picture had been and was gone, the caption remained. It read, *Mr. and Mrs. Meredith!* and then, in parentheses *(We didn't know 'twas taken!)*

Duff sucked his cheek, felt a twinge of embarrassed pity, and then he looked at Mr. Moriarity once more, fondly. He snapped his finger at the page, clicking his nail on Moriarity's pictured chest. He went back to where his other hand was still keeping a place.

Four pictures had been on this page, too, and one of

187

them was gone. The time was much earlier, nearer the turn of the century. At the left, on top, two women in long skirts and shirtwaists, with Howard Chandler Christy hair, stood drooping gracefully against each other on a lawn. The caption, *Mother and Aunt Edie*. Duff studied them. Obviously sisters, both had long oval faces and slightly protruding eyes, startled-looking. Both had thin noses and thick brows and narrow little mouths, parted in ladylike simpers. Was one simper less easy than the other? Duff couldn't tell. One had a jabot, the other a mannish necktie.

Below, the one with the jabot drooped gracefully against a man in a dark suit whose legs were planted in that ancient and elegant stance for the virile which required the feet to make a right angle, and one thigh to turn out, as if it belonged to a ballet dancer. He had his arms folded, too, and his mustache, like a plant from a hanging basket, hung over his mouth. The background was the same lawn, although now the corner of a perambulator could be seen, just behind them, from which fell a froth of fringe on a cover of some sort. Caption, *Uncle Arthur and Aunt Edie*. Ah, yes.

But the third picture was the one that had stopped him. Duff bent his eyes on it. This was another woman entirely. This time she sat on the grass in a puddle of white skirts. Caption, *Nursey*. Yes, she must have been a nurse. Indeed, Duff thought he spotted a thermometer in her pocket. A starched, sober-eyed woman, sitting with a straight back and with her feet decorously hidden. In this picture, also, he could see a corner of the same perambulator, with the same fringe falling in the same folds. Behind the white-clad woman

188

there was a round flower bed.

Duff studied every shadow, every fold, every leaf and blade of grass.

He sighed and looked above, to where the picture was gone. One of its little black corner holders was still there, loose and sliding. The caption, *Baby Edarth*.

Duff shook his head and looked back at Edie and her jabot.

Baby Edarth was gone.

Edie was gone, deceased, he supposed, 1940.

Uncle Arthur would be very old now if alive. Mother was gone, probably. Nursey? Nursey could be somebody's mother, by now. Somebody's mother was something, somewhere. Duff sifted his recollections vaguely. He ran the pages through to the end of the album. None of these people appeared again.

Instead, there was Ralph. Ralph was a fat baby, then a thin urchin, then a middle-weight boy. He was there in all his doings, moods, seasons, stages, until he had been fifteen or so. Then there were no more Ralphs, no more pages in the album.

There had been gaps and sometimes his name in white ink, but no picture of Edgar Meredith at all.

Duff went back to the page with the jabot. He brooded.

It was coming clear. His mind, released from prison or wherever it had been, leaped, guessed, checked, clicked, meshed, and wove the answer.

"Mr. Duff!" Eve was shaking him by the shoulder. "Mr. Duff, are you all right?"

Duff murmured in his throat.

"You've been sitting here so still!" she cried. "I came in five minutes ago, and you haven't seen me or said anything. I'm sorry. I began to worry. I didn't know . . ."

"I'm sorry," he said. He looked down at the album in his hands. There was no dust on it.

"Did you find it? The picture of Denis? I think there *is* one. Maybe I can . . ."

"No." Duff stood up with the album tight under his arm. He looked down at her. She was tense. He felt a great pity for her, momentarily. "Why did you take all of your husband's pictures out?" he asked her gently. "What did you do with them? Throw them away?"

"Yes."

"Why?"

"Because they made me think of old times I would rather forget," she said harshly.

"Because they were good or because they were bad?"

"Whichever they were. It doesn't matter." Her hand on her throat pinched and pulled the skin. Her eyes kept his defiantly.

"May I borrow this album for a day or two?"

"What!"

"Please."

She moistened her lips. Her eyes flew frantically to the corners of his face, combing it for explanation. "But what for?"

"I need it."

"Well, of course, if you need it . . ." Her other hand went out behind her, reaching for the back of a chair. He couldn't tell what her imagination was doing.

"Thanks very much," he said charmingly. "You've been very helpful. I'm very grateful." He moved on a wave of "verys."

"Why, that's all right, Mr. Duff," she tried to say. But she had to whisper it.

Duff swung back through the gate and turned across the lawn toward the front of the Moriarity house. No one was on the terrace now, and no blue figure, he knew, worked among the cabbages.

He got to his car and put the album down beside him with a pat of satisfaction. MacDougal Duff was himself again.

He drove directly to the police station, spoke briefly to Robin, who was there although Pring was not, asked to see a certain exhibit, and made off with it. He told Robin to stop around at Mary's later this afternoon, about five, and maybe . . . Robin spit his gum all the way out and said sure, they'd be there. Sure thing.

Duff then went to Schrafft's on Main Street, got into the telephone booth, called Maguire's number, got a number to call, and got Maguire.

"Duff. Go ahead. You're in Haytonville?"

"Yeah." Maguire wasn't surprised. He never had been yet. "It's Mrs. Meredith's aunt, all right."

"What's her first name?"

"Edith." Duff smiled to himself. "Edith Norden."

"Norden!"

"Yeah, Mrs. Meredith's mother was Norden, too, married a distant cousin with the same name."

Duff clicked his tongue. "Go on."

"Edith Norden Sims. Mrs. A. Christopher Sims. That's how they got her down in the records, both ways."

"A for Arthur?"

"Yeah, A for Arthur. She was committed in 1919.

Died, 1940. Natural causes. Emily Brown found out what ailed her. Told Edgar Meredith. He left his wife and baby, scared of it. Thought his kids would turn out nutty. That's your feud."

"Good work. What else?"

"Lemme see. Nobody liked her much, Miss Brown, I mean, but she came and went, always visiting. And I don't find anything seems like it calls for murder. Not yet. Couldn't get much about her and this Moriarity, though there was an old lady across the hall remembers Brown felt cool about him. She don't know much. Could be Brown didn't like any of her friends' husbands much."

"Could be," said Duff cheerfully. "Go on."

"That guy exists, all right. That guy that got away. Up at White Plains. They got him back last night. Found him in Paterson, New Jersey. Severson. His right name's Patrini. No soap on the safe deposit."

Duff grunted. "What did you see in her New York apartment?"

"Only one room and bath. Not so much in there. She never stayed long. Nothing homey about it. All the time visiting, she was, like I said. Nothing in her past turned up yet."

"Did you find any photographs?" asked Duff.

"Yeah, yeah. Her mother. Sad-looking old lady, gray hair, dead now. And her old man, dead years ago. Couple of snaps of a picnic, don't know what people. Cabinet job on herself, pretty well touched up, I should say. Picture of a man, right in with the rest. If she was sweet on him, well . . . she never had him framed." Duff chuckled. Maguire was a little jewel. "Picture of a bunch of people and some palm trees. California, I guess. Picture of a baby."

"An old-fashioned baby?"

"Yeah, pretty old-fashioned."

"Sitting on the grass?"

"Yeah, that's right. Bonnet and a lotta clothes."

"Boy or girl?"

"My God," said Maguire, "who can say?"

"White kid shoe with tassel?'

"Yeah, yeah, only one shoe showing."

"That's it," said Duff. "O.K."

"Wait. Say, I got nothing on any Haggerty. Not a trace."

"Never mind," said Duff. "Go home. I'll call you later."

Duff walked back into the restaurant. He was still carrying the album. He ordered lunch and afterward sat long and quietly in a corner, staring at the murals of the Huguenots landing with even his historian's eyes blind to them.

He was laying the ghost. At last he remembered the odd gesture Haggerty had made, that night when Duff had turned him away at the front door.

A waitress, who had thought the gentleman in the corner to be dozing with his eyes open, nearly dropped her tray at the sudden beautiful warm smile he gave her.

He made another phone call.

It was three in the afternoon when he came back to Mary's house. Everyone was out of doors. Mary wandered dreamily among her plants, snipping here

193

and there, not really working at anything. Taffy, looking like a little lady-doll above the shoulders, with her braids pinned up on top of her head but wearing only a pair of red gingham overalls, was playing by the pool. She and Davey had a game.

Duff went over to see what they were shrieking about. It seemed they each had a piece of shingle, boats, they said. The point was to roil up the water by beating it with a stick so that one boat or the other was driven across the pool. Davey sat at the rim with his knees drawn up to his chin, looking like a pixie, and whammed away, let the spray fall where it may. A good deal of it fell on Duff. He retired to a drier distance. He had a clear premonition that sooner or later Davey would fall in.

Taffy, pink in the face with delight, looked as if she had never been sick or troubled in her life. Mitch and another little girl were up in the apple tree, chattering like jays.

Dinny had washed her hair and lay on her stomach on the grass, her white mop over her eyes like a terrier. She had a book. The noise of hammering came sporadically from the stable, adding the pleasant sound of someone at work to the pervading sense of busy peace.

Duff drifted to where Mary was and offered his premonition about Davey. Mary agreed that he would probably fall in, said he usually did. She beamed upon him. "Where were you? We set your place for lunch. Have you had any?" He nodded. "You did go to Eve's, didn't you? She called me. Did you find what you wanted?"

"And more," he said.

She straightened her back, frowned, let a moment of silence go by. Then she said, "You're different."

"I am a new man."

Mary closed her scissors. "Why?"

"I'm in the classical position of one who knows all and can't prove it." He smiled. She said nothing but looked sharply into his eyes. "It'll be all right," he said. "Are the doctor and Miss Avery going to Eve's for tea?"

"I don't know," Mary turned to snip off a dying blossom. "Mustn't I ask questions?" she said, with her back turned.

"I'm going to ask the questions," he told her, explaining himself, as if she'd understand. "Not of you, Mary. But I'm going to surrender the luxury of being always right. I'm going to trot my unproved guesses right out into the open. This is no time to insist on being any mastermind. I hope to smoke out the truth by attacking, proof or no proof, with all my suspicions. Let me not, this time, wait for another murder to prove my case."

"Another . . . !" She was alarmed.

"Never mind. Just believe me. Your children had nothing to do with it."

She believed him, and she sighed. He saw her count her chicks with a sweep of her eyes around the garden. For the first time, she began to thank him.

"I wonder what I can ever do . . ."

"Give me one of Taffy's roses."

She snipped him a quaint striped blossom. She held it out. "Rosa Mundi," he murmured. "Rose of the world."

"But you like the others better, don't you?" They

strolled into the rose garden proper.

"What do you call them?" He didn't care what she called them. He was very happy. She had believed him.

"This is Christopher Stone," Mary touched a red rose. "There's Alice Stern."

"Who?"

"That white rose."

Duff bent to sniff a yellow flower. "That's Mrs. Pierre S. Dupont," said Mary.

"Where!"

"Right under your nose." She was laughing.

"My word!" said Duff. "Are flowers people?"

"It's funny, sometimes. When it comes to tulips . . . ! I've got the Reverend Ewbank and Ellen Willmott in the same . . . bed." Mary buttoned her lips together, and the thin dimple trembled in and out of her cheek.

"Mary," he said.

Mary tipped her head to listen, but he had nothing to add and her eyes fell. "Look, if you're going to take to calling me Mary," she said, and the blue gaze was back, "as you have, you know, what shall I call you? Mac?" She wrinkled her nose.

Dinny, whom they had forgotten, rolled over. "Jean Barney's got a scotty dog. She calls him Dougal. He's awful cute."

"Dinny!" Mary blushed. But Duff, being himself again, showed no sign of embarrassment. He stood beside her, a tall man with a quiet certainty, an easy balance about him. He looked sidewise at Dinny, meeting her dark defiant eyes under the white wild mop of her hair.

Then his rare smile transformed his long, wise, and rather melancholy face into one gayer and younger and, as he looked down at Mary again, quite reckless with affection. "Call me anything you like," he said. "Hey you, will do. But no six children or wild horses, either, are going to keep me from thinking 'Mary,' or saying why, someday."

He saw Dinny put her under lip over her upper lip so that her fat face looked as if it were locking in an explosion.

"Will you stay for supper?" Mary murmured to a rosebush.

"Gladly."

"Will you . . . be at the doctor's tonight?"

"I don't know."

Dinny got up with elaborate grace. She stood still a moment, then swept back her hair with her arm, bent at the elbow. She swayed, giving for a moment the illusion of slenderness, of woe. Then Duff could have sworn that the eyes under the bare arm, although they were wide open, nevertheless winked at him. She slipped off toward the stable.

Duff stood alone with Mary among the flowers.

Davey fell in.

Taffy danced on the grass. Mitch, landing on her toes and bouncing like a soap bubble, fell out of the apple tree, followed more clumsily by her friend. Paul, Dinny, and Alfie came tearing around from the stable, uttering false cries of concern. None of these three big ones looked at MacDougal Duff.

They all fished Davey out and hung him on the terrace to dry. Mary took his shoes off, although Davey said he liked them squilchy, and besides, he felt a fish in one and wouldn't it die? Mary said if there were a fish it might, but there was no fish.

Mitch and her friend drifted, in little impulsive rushes, back to their tree. But Paul and the twins did not disappear about their business. The scene became a little unreal. Taffy and Davey, unself-conscious, deep in the golden "now" of childhood, discussed the ways of fish, and Mary seemed to be listening with a dreamy smile. Neither Dinny nor Paul moved at all, but Alfie spoke as suddenly as if they had nudged him.

"Hey, Mr. Duff," he cried in his bubbling way, "listen, there *is* a picture of Dad. Up in the turtle-back trunk. Upstairs."

"Is there?" said Mary slowly, looking up.

"That's right!" said Dinny in slow surprise. "Sure there is."

Followed a little silence. Water dripped off Davey on the stones. Nobody said, "I'll get it, shall I?" It was a curious little omission. Duff had seen these kids eager to fetch and carry for their mother. Their normal sunny willingness seemed muffled.

Duff lay low.

Mary said, at last. "That's right, maybe there is." She turned to Duff. "Do you want to see it, now?"

"Why, yes, we might go and see if it's there," he said lazily.

"All right," said Mary.

So they climbed the stairs, and the kids let them go, remaining quietly below. They reached the third-floor hall, to which no light came save through the open door to the boys' room. Mary put her hand on the door to the middle storeroom, opened it.

She screamed.

Duff pressed behind her, and his arms went out. She

198

turned in his arms and he held her, looking over her shoulder at the rocking chair.

It was rocking.

Alone, by itself in the gloom, it was rocking violently, as if someone had only just got up and that quickly. "Someone's up here! Someone in the house!" Mary trembled.

Duff held her closer and put his chin gently down on her dark hair. "Hush," he soothed. "It's nothing."

"N-nothing! But . . ."

"Hush. It's only a ghost. Don't be afraid." She turned her mouth against his shoulder, whimpering. Duff moved his hand on her back in the gentlest caress.

The big kids were banging up the stairs behind them. Duff didn't turn. He held onto Mary. "Only the Hessian ghost," he said cheerfully. "Probably was sitting there rocking his head to sleep. Or didn't they chop his head off, Dinny? I forget."

Mary wiggled away. He let her go. The rocking chair was trembling to repose. Mary's face was a study in pink bewilderment. The kids were looking very blank. Nobody said a word. They were suspended in silence. The chair settled and was still.

Then from below, Mitch yelled, "Mommy. Companee!" Her healthy shout broke the spell. Mary looked wildly at her children's faces, put her head down, and ran for the stairs.

CHAPTER 15

The doctor was saying, "Let's not go, darling. I'll call her up. A doctor never has to keep social engagements. Please . . ."

"I'm sure I don't care about going," said Constance coolly. She stood in the middle of Mary's living room with an air of faint disdain, as if she saw no chair quite worth sitting in. "You accepted for us, Norry. If you can make an excuse," she shrugged. "It isn't necessary to offend the woman."

"She won't be offended," began the doctor, "she . . ." Mary stood in the arch. "Ah, Mary. Is Mr. Duff here?"

Mary nodded.

"He left a message. We came right over."

"Aren't you going to Eve's?"

"Frankly, I just don't feel like it," said the doctor. "Damned if I do. I'm more interested to know what Duff wants. Do you know?"

Mary said to Mitch, "Run upstairs and tell Mr. Duff the doctor's here to see him, will you, hon?" She looked at her jeans. "If you're not going, then it isn't a party. I think I'll run over a minute, just as I am."

"You explain, then," said Dr. Christenson quickly. "Tell her none of us can come. Say Duff wants us, eh?"

"I'll tell her you just don't feel like it," said Mary casually.

"Don't let her do that!"

"Why?" said Mary, turning and looking into Constance's face. "It isn't necessary to lie to her."

"Tell her anything," said the doctor desperately, "but get out of it and come back and let's see what Duff has on his mind." He ran a hand through his thin hair. "Will you, Mary?"

Mary cocked an ear toward the stairs and flew.

The doctor sat down. Constance looked at him with vague displeasure. Then she, too, sat down in her decorous well-bred way, gracefully erect, the ankle neatly placed. She was in ice blue today.

Duff bowed.

The kids blew by in the hall, behind him. The garden door slammed.

"I got your message," the doctor began.

Duff glanced at his watch. "It's early," he murmured. "Pring won't be here until five."

"Well," said the doctor, "shall we—er—wait? Or what?"

"What are we waiting for?" said Constance crisply.

Duff stood by a table, turning over the leaves of a nurseryman's catalogue. "I had some things to say," he stated mildly.

"To me?" Her lip curled.

Duff didn't answer. He was looking down at the colored pictures under his hand.

201

The doctor said, "It must be important," as if to soothe his lady. Then to Duff, "Is there anything you can tell us before the rest—er—?"

"Oh, yes, I think so." Duff was annoyingly vague and dawdling.

"What's in your mind?" said the doctor. He folded his hands over his stomach, elbows on their chair arms. He leaned back. " *'Lay on, Mac Duff; and damn'd be him that first cries, Hold, enough!'* Eh?"

Constance took out her compact and studied her eyes.

Duff raised his head and something in the quiet of his pose caused her to snap the compact shut and put it away.

"There's a better quotation from the same play," said Duff, soberly. " *'Look like the innocent flower, but be the serpent under't.'* "

"Act I, Scene 5," said Constance glibly with an insulting effect. "Lady Macbeth, isn't it?"

Duff pushed the open catalogue away. "Did you know there was a pink rose called, of all things, the Doctor?" Dr. Christenson's eyebrows flew. "That's an omen, perhaps. Dr. Christenson, you had a motive, you know. The fattest motive I have found, so far."

"*I* had!"

"Oh, yes, to murder Brownie." Duff turned to the woman who hadn't moved or spoken. "I wonder," he said, "if, yesterday, when you spoke so vigorously about bad blood, as you called it . . . Did you then know that Mrs. Meredith's own aunt had died in an asylum?"

"No," said Constance. Then, belatedly, "Did she, really?"

Duff said, "Dr. Christenson wants very much to marry you."

"Why, I assume as much," she said, brushing her skirt.

The doctor said, "Look here . . ."

Duff held up his hand. "I found an old album," he said dreamily, "and I read quite a lot on one of its pages. On an old page. For instance, there was Aunt Edie, the one who went mad, y'know. In a jabot, she was. And Uncle Arthur, too. Her husband. Arthur Christopher Sims, his name. There were two other pictures, taken that very day. I know, because the same perambulator was in two of them, behind the parents, behind the nurse. The same fringed blanket, falling out in the same folds. And the nurse, mind you, sat on the grass, in front of a round flower bed. A round flower bed.

"The flowers spoke. The daisies told. Don't you see? The flowers were in a certain stage of development that day, that year. Also, the shadows fell the same, in that hour.

"But the fourth picture, the one of the baby, taken then and there, you see, because of the flower bed, was gone. It was gone because Brownie stole it, Sunday afternoon. Oh, yes. I have it here. The police let me take it. You can see where those black corners have been stuck across. Look. Out of no box of old stuff, doctor. But out of Eve's album.

"Yes, that's little Edarth. Sentimental, eh? To make up such a name. Child of Edith and Arthur." Duff tapped the picture. "Quaint." He dropped his dreamy manner. "But you say this is a picture of yourself, Dr. Christenson?"

The doctor barely looked at it. "Yes. Yes, I . . . But she had my picture a long time. You must be . . ."

"Not mistaken," said Duff. "The flowers, you see? Those four pictures made a perfect chain. Even the sisters, did I tell you? Eve's mother and her aunt, own sisters. So much alike. No, Dr. Christenson, it's clear enough. You are, in fact, little Edarth.

"Yes, I think you are Arthur's son. You made it Christopher's son, or Christenson. More sentiment, I suppose. Was your second name Norden? Norris is close." Duff skipped a beat. "And then, of course, you are Edie's son, too, are you not? And Edie, as they used to say, went mad."

No one spoke.

So Duff went on.

"Brownie knew all about Edie. Indeed, she'd used the same scandalous story once before. I can imagine, when she went to Eve's house Sunday for the ice collar, and, waiting there in the sitting room, picked up the album, blew off the dust, and opened it, with what surprise she found your picture. Oh, she knew that picture. She had another copy of it, herself. In New York now. Yes, it's there.

"Now, therefore, she would know at sight of it that you must be Eve's first cousin, and also what your heritage must be."

Duff put the picture in his pocket as if he had ended that chapter.

"Brownie rather fancied you, didn't she, doctor? Wasn't she a little possessive, shall we say? She'd loaned you money—oh, no, it wasn't the money that mattered to either of you—but she'd been the old friend, good sport, comrade. Oh, I can imagine. But now you were going to introduce your fiancee, the wealthy and beautiful Miss Avery.

"And you didn't think Brownie could resist telling your fiancee all about Aunt Edie."

Silence.

"Well, I think you were right about that," Duff said. "Sounds like a typical reaction. Although I don't suppose Brownie knew as well as you do Miss Avery's very decided views on that subject. Did she tell you, upstairs, in Mary's room? Brownie. Did she say that she'd found out? Did she say, 'So you're Eve's cousin, Norry! Why ever didn't you tell me?' "

The doctor groaned.

"*You* knew it would lose you Constance, whom you love and want, and lose you her money and her prestige as well."

"That's not . . ." The doctor choked.

Duff closed his eyes a moment. "Of course you did try to telephone and call off the evening. But she was busy with the henhouse. So it had to be tragedy."

Constance had not moved yet.

"I suppose you have a good reason," said Dr. Christenson humbly, "for doing this to me."

"Sufficient reason," Duff said.

He flipped the catalogue closed. He did not look at the woman.

"It *was* tragedy, you know, in the real sense," he said quietly. "Because if you'd understood, you needn't have done it."

Constance said, her voice ringing out, "Norry, don't worry. I shan't believe any of this, of course."

205

"You see?" said Duff softly.

"See? See what?" The doctor's eyes were wild behind his glasses.

"She doesn't wish to believe it," said Duff. "Miss Constance Avery. And she wouldn't have believed it or been lost, at all. As a matter of fact, Doctor, you are her last hope. But you didn't know that. You couldn't see Miss Constance Avery for what she is, a singularly unattractive woman, Doctor, from whom, I imagine, men have run like steers in the past, in spite of her money. She is . . . deficient. She has no appeal. There is a certain coldness. Oh, she knows. She has become, if you can see beyond that front, a little bit desperate. You are the only man left, I daresay, whom she can persuade to accept her on her own terms, as if *she* were the exclusive, persnickety, fastidious prize."

Duff paused. Then he burst out, as if this were too obvious, "Why, good Lord, the woman's an old maid, as they used to say. Born to it, too. Some women are."

Constance's pale face was pale no longer. She looked like a Fury, sitting there in ice blue, her hands shaking in rage. But a rage terribly controlled.

"She lets you worship," said Duff. "I've noticed. But have you ever felt the slightest warmth? Can't you tell that her desire for a husband is conventional, not real, not of the earth? Oh, it's a desire. It's a rebellion. It denies her own lack. That's why it's so strong. That's why she'll never let you go. Even now. Will you, Miss Avery?"

Constance said nothing.

But the doctor began to laugh.

"Norry!" said Constance, like a whiplash. Then suddenly she wailed like a child. "Norry . . ."

206

The doctor laughed so hard he nearly choked. "Oh, God," he said, "maybe I should have let her go to the tea party. Oh, God . . ."

Duff lost all languor. "Where's Mary!" But Constance was looking at the doctor as if she would have killed him, had she the means, in this moment. Her eyes were narrow, her teeth bared. She was not pretty.

"Where's Mary!"

Duff was out on the terrace somehow with no sensation of having moved at all.

"Where's Mary!"

Dinny said, "Mother's gone over to Aunt Eve's."

Duff began to run.

"Please have some coffee with me, Mary. We'll have it iced. It's warm, isn't it? Or am I just upset?"

"Did Mr. Duff upset you?" Mary sat down on a porch chair and lit a cigarette.

"Well, he did and he didn't," Eve said. "I'll tell you." She went into the kitchen. Mary smoked and looked across the garden. Eve came back with a tray, two tall glasses, a plate of little cakes, sugar and cream.

"I wasn't going to have anything fancy. That cream's frozen, of all things. So they couldn't come? I'll bet they didn't want to come." Her auburn eyes were shrewd.

Mary said carelessly, "Oh, Mr. Duff wanted to talk to them."

"He scared me," said Eve. "He really did, Mary. I thought he was dead. He was sitting there like a dead man. Honestly. Finally I couldn't stand it. I shook him. He came out of it all right."

"What was the matter? Was he . . . thinking, you mean?"

"Maybe. But he looked *dead!*" Eve twitched. "I never saw anybody sit so still. Not living. The coffee will be through in a minute. Then he took my album."

"He did? Why?"

"I don't *know*. I don't *know*. I can't imagine." Eve gnawed her fingers. "I'm just as glad she didn't come here today."

"I wouldn't weep, if I were you," said Mary.

Eve's lids fell. "You knew about Aunt Edie, didn't you?"

Mary flicked ashes, said quietly, "Yes, I couldn't help knowing. My mother and your mother . . ."

"You never spoke of it?"

"No. Never."

Eve sucked her breath in.

"I didn't think you wanted it talked about," Mary said. "Besides, there wasn't anything to say. Just something that happened quite a while ago. I won't ever talk about it, Eve. You can be sure."

"Yes," said Eve, "I know you won't, Mary." Her eyes flashed. "You do see why, don't you? It's because Ralph mustn't ever know! He doesn't need to, Mary. Why should he? I've watched him. He's all right. I even had him examined twice, when he was littler, without . . . you know . . . I pretended I just thought it was wise. And he's fine. As long as nobody tells him . . . He is really just as strong and steady . . . He needn't ever have to worry, so why should I tell him when he'd be sure to worry then? Just as those doctors would have found something if they'd known . . . if I'd put it in their heads. I don't *believe* a lot of what they say. Oh, *I've*

208

worried, God knows. And then, sometimes I think what if the things he's got to go through now . . . what if he can't stand them?" She sobbed, and Mary touched her shoulder.

"Get the coffee, Eve. Ralph's all right. Edgar was a pretty stolid fellow. It might not even do Ralph any harm if he did find out. Remember that."

"Oh, Edgar . . . he was so damn' stolid he nearly drove me wild!" Eve cried. "But Ralph mustn't find out," she muttered.

She went off to the kitchen again and came back in a minute with a bowl of brown ice cubes and the coffeepot.

Mary nibbled a cake. "What makes you think of your Aunt Edie?"

"Oh, what *she* said."

"Constance?"

"Yes."

"Don't pay her any mind."

"I could . . ." began Eve darkly. She rattled ice cubes into the glasses and poured the hot coffee over them. "One of these days . . ." She stopped herself again. "It's Ralph, though," she muttered. "I worry so."

"Of course you do," said Mary. "What did Mr. Duff *say?*"

"He didn't say much. Why did he want to see a picture of Denis?"

"*I* don't know," said Mary.

"Maybe he didn't. Maybe he just wanted . . ."

"What?"

"That Brownie!" said Eve. "She couldn't even die. Oh, Mary, I'm so sorry about it all. Oh, God, why is life such a damn mess?"

"I don't know that it is," said Mary calmly. "Sometimes I think it's a pretty fine thing, as far as it goes."

"It doesn't go very far," said Eve bitterly. "That's a comfort. It ends, I guess. Don't you like iced coffee, Mary? Have you had sugar? Cream?"

"It's fine, thanks." Mary took the glass. Eve rattled the cubes in hers. Her eyes glittered. Mary wondered if she were going to cry.

"You're doing too much, Eve. Please don't keep on at the hospital. I think it's too much for you."

"Good thing I was there, just the same," said Eve darkly.

"What do you mean?" Mary felt frightened. She lifted her glass.

"No. No, nothing. I—Who's that!"

Duff came over the gate as if it were a hurdle, sailing across in a leap like a dancer's, scarcely breaking his long running stride.

"What's happened now!" Eve's claw went for her own throat.

"Heaven knows!" Mary took a long swig of iced coffee as if to fortify herself.

Eve's teeth rattled on the glass. She, too, drank some.

Duff leaped to the porch and knocked her glass out of Mary's hand. It broke on the floor. The brown ice slid and left a glistening trail. His fingers hurt her shoulders. She cried out. He was looking into her face with the most terrible anxiety.

"Mr. Duff!" she gasped.

"Mary, darling, have they killed you? How do you feel? How do you feel!"

"I'd feel fine," said Mary, "if you'd let me go, please."

Duff took his hands away and they were shaking. He looked at Eve.

He said, "Are you sure?" in a dead voice.

"What on earth's the matter?" Eve Meredith cried. "Of course she's all right. Why wouldn't she be?"

Duff gave her a weary look and collapsed on the steps. He said nothing. His long hands hung off his wrists. He was like a big dog.

In a moment Mary leaned over and said gently, "What did you think was wrong?" Her voice forgave and understood. She felt sorry.

"I thought . . ." he panted. He rubbed a hand over his face for a moment.

"You must have been mistaken," said Mary. "There's nothing wrong here."

Duff made no answer.

The kids came pouring through the gate, even Davey. Duff got up and stood over the tray. He examined the cakes. "You've eaten some of these?" He poked at the ice cubes. "Why are they brown?"

"I always do that in the summer," explained Eve in a rapid patter. "I just put the leftover coffee from breakfast in the ice tray. So then I have them all ready. It makes iced coffee so much better. Otherwise, it gets diluted."

"I see."

"I got the idea out of a magazine, years ago. I . . ."

"Yes. Yes." Duff put his finger in the sugar, tasted it. "You take sugar?"

"Of course. We both did. There's nothing wrong with the . . ."

Duff tasted the cream. He looked at the bowl of ice again. "You put coffee in the ice tray early?"

"Right after breakfast."

"Mommy," said Mitch.

"Mother—"

Duff smiled at last, down into the six worried faces. "She's all right," he said cheerfully. "I made a mistake, I guess. That's all."

"Boy, boy, oh, boy," said Alfie in a moment. "Can *you* move!"

"Can *you* run!" said Paul. "Jeepers."

"Come on home," said Dinny. "Mother, please come home." The little ones looked frightened, and all their round eyes implored her. So Mary went, convoyed by her young, walking slowly among them as if she were a little dazed.

Duff stood a minute. Then he looked at Eve.

"Why don't you come, too?" he said. "You don't want to be alone, do you?"

"No," said Eve. "No."

The doctor held Constance in his arms. "It's all right, all *right!*" he said. His eyes could see, through the window, the procession that was coming. "It's all right, darling. Don't cry."

Constance wasn't crying. She could see through the window, too. "We needn't stay here," she said.

"We'd better."

"No."

"Don't worry, Connie," he soothed. "Duff's only using me to trap somebody else, I think. Wait . . ."

She moved and looked up at him. "It's all right," he

212

said. "Why, my darling, it will have to be all right, now!"

"But I'd like to go," she said a little coldly.

"No," he smiled at her. "We'll stay."

She said no more. She got out her compact. On the hand holding it, her knuckles were white.

The front doorbell rang.

Paul swept through the hall to the front door before the doctor could get there. Pring and Robin stood outside and behind them, looking as if he were about to make a deep bow, was Mr. F. X. Haggerty.

"Looking for Mr. Duff . . ."

"He's here."

"Mr. Duff?"

"Sure. Come in."

Duff faced them all. The kids and Mary, the doctor, Constance, the two detectives, and Haggerty, and Eve.

"Well, what goes on?" said Pring stolidly. "Anything happen?"

"No," said MacDougal Duff. "Nothing happened."

Somewhere, upstairs, there was a distant crash.

CHAPTER 16

What was that!"

"Something fall?"

"Who's up there?"

"Nobody," cried Mary. "There can't be anybody. We're all here!"

Eye met eye.

Duff said smoothly, "Suppose we go see who is up there? Come on, Pring. You, too, Robin. And you, boys, if you please. Alfie and Paul. Doctor, will you watch these stairs? Dinny, show Mr. Haggerty the back stairs, please."

"Oh, I know," said Haggerty. "I happen . . ."

But the boys had snapped into action. They started up, and Duff and the detectives followed fast.

"The third floor, I imagine," Duff said. "It usually is."

Robin shifted his gum, and they went on. But there

was nobody on the third floor. It slept in dusty warmth, all of it, empty, still innocent.

"What the deuce?" Pring shoved his hat back on his head.

"Sounded like a window," said Duff. "These windows have to be propped up. No sash weights. Isn't that so?"

The boys murmured yes. They hadn't done any boyish chattering. They were very silent boys.

Duff peered about some more.

"Hey," said Robin from the front storeroom. "Look here."

They gathered around the window, which was closed. Robin pushed it up. It opened to the street front. Outside, on a little flare of shingles that crossed the face of the house, there was a splash of water. The western sun was still hot, and it slanted this way. Water on those shingles should have dried quickly.

Duff leaned out. There were, he noticed, two nails standing out from the shingles, about an inch apart, and all around them the shingles were wet. He felt a wriggling body hanging out beside him. Paul had Alfie by the heels. Alfie was reaching down to feel of the wetness. His finger started toward his mouth.

Suddenly Duff slapped him hard, on the hand. "Don't taste it!" Alfie let out a howl of surprise, and Paul hauled indignantly at his legs.

"Don't touch it again." Duff bent a stern glance on Alfie's red astonished face. "What did you do with the rest of them?"

"Huh?"

"Give up. I know. All, see." Duff included Paul. "Come on." Alfie was goggling. Paul looked a little red, too. "Where are those other coffee-flavored ice cubes? Speak up, my lads, because they're poisoned, you know."

"P-poisoned!"

"Listen," said Paul, "we didn't . . ."

"I know. I know. You didn't. But where are they? Quick."

"We put them down the toilet," Alfie confessed.

"And the tray?"

"We washed it and put it back."

"In your mother's icebox?"

"Yeah, sure."

"But you got it from Eve's? Didn't you?"

"They fit, all right," said Paul. "Same kind of icebox."

Duff turned to Pring. "Soak up some of that moisture on a handkerchief. Here's a clean one. See if we can get enough to have analyzed. All we need is a trace. Try it."

Robin was already half out the window.

"Why? What is it?" said Pring flatly.

"Nicotine, I imagine."

Pring whistled.

"The Moriarity kids," said Duff, "have been hoaxing me. At least four of them have. Maybe five. I think these boys heard you say it must have been an inside job. Nobody here but the family. So they were going to have us hunting a mysterious somebody who must be hiding in this house. They had me doing it, too. For a while. We've had a lot of fun. Ghost stories, and everything. Fun's fun. Still . . ." Duff staggered a little.

"You saved your mother's life, today," he said to the

216

boys, "when I would have been too late. So all is forgiven." With an effort, he smiled at them. "Please believe me . . ."

The boys murmured and shifted their feet.

"Listen," said Pring, "what is this? Do you mind?"

Duff told him, "There was a coffee ice cube, such as Mrs. Meredith always has handy for making iced coffee. One of the kids got the inspiration—"

"Alfie," murmured Paul. It was his sense of justice. Alfie had been smart and must have the credit.

"Put it between those nails," said Duff. "Look. See them? Brace a stick there, on a long slant to the window, holding it up. Everybody goes downstairs, hangs around in full sight. The sun shines. The ice melts. The stick slips. Bang! The stick goes over, down among the bushes. It seems as if somebody up here has closed a window.

"But that's not all," he continued. "We arrive. If we see the wet spot, we might be bright enough to think of ice. But—it tastes like black coffee! Ah-ha, we deduce, so the mysterious dweller in the attic was just getting rid of a little leftover coffee after his snack and the window slipped out of his hand. Oh, yes, we'd have noticed it was coffee. Alfie wasn't taking any chances. He was going to make that discovery for us, in case we were too dumb."

"You're not so dumb," said Alfie cheerfully.

"But how come? Whatdaya mean, poison?" Pring and Paul demanded. Paul looked angry, as if evil had no right to intrude upon a merry prank, and Pring looked both grim and doubtful.

"I *believe* it's poisoned," Duff said. "I ran my legs

217

off, believing that. I can be wrong."

Robin pulled his head in at the window and rolled up the handkerchief. "We can find out, I guess."

"You kids stole Mrs. Meredith's ice tray?" Pring asked them as if he needed to start over again.

"Yeah," said Paul rapidly, standing up to the question. It was obvious he felt no guilt but sought the truth as they did. "We didn't think of it until too late to make our own, and anyhow, Mr. Duff mighta got into *our* icebox. So we took Mom's coffeepot and fixed another tray and changed them."

"When?" Duff asked.

"About two-thirty."

"You turned Eve's icebox up, I suppose?"

"All the way."

"Yeah, we hadda," chimed Alfie. "Paul figgered . . ."

"But listen, it took all that time to melt?" Pring looked doubtful still.

"It's four-thirty," said Robin with a fat frown. "We got here early."

"Naturally," said Paul, "we didn't fix the window and the stick until Mr. Duff went back downstairs a little while ago. Of course, the coffee ice was melted some already. But we had some other ice in a pail. We'd kept it cool. We'd figgered it out roughly."

"Say, listen," cried Alfie, "it worked, didn't it? It would have been *good!*"

"It was good," Duff said. "I assure you, it could have fooled me. It would have fooled me all to pieces. Thank God you fooled somebody else. Well, shall we go down now?"

They all obeyed his suggestion like puppets or people who moved in a daze.

"Yeah, but who put the poison in Mrs. Meredith's ice tray?" said Pring, abruptly, halfway down, as if he'd just remembered that this was the question.

"I'll tell you what I think," Duff said, "when we get downstairs. It will be only what I think."

"You think good," said Alfie.

"Yeah," said Paul.

CHAPTER 17

There is no one in the house," Duff made his
announcement to them all, "except those of us here in
this room now. Won't you all sit down somewhere?"

Mary was already seated, there in her living room,
on the red couch where Brownie had died. She had
Davey under one wing and Taffy under the other.
Mitch, who leaned over behind them, kept one hand on
Mary's shoulder to which, now and then, Mary bent
her cheek. She hadn't enough wings to go around.
Dinny, too, was curled up like a spring the other side
of her littlest brother, and the big boys, marching as
one, went directly across and joined the family
portrait.

Seven Moriaritys made a quiet phalanx. Solid and
indivisible. It was clear that they stood for each other
against the world.

Dr. Christenson and Constance sat down across the
room.

Eve Meredith, lonely and tense, crouched in a chair

by the cold fireplace and watched on all sides, as if she were an animal at bay.

Pring and Robin arranged themselves, by some instinct, between the rest and the hall. Mr. Haggerty put himself, with a meek and humble air, into a corner where he remained, quiet as a mouse, with his notebook handy.

Duff let the silence settle, like dust.

"I am going to tell you what I have been thinking," he said at last, "and we shall see where it leads us. This is what I believe—part guess, part intuition, part logic, part faith. And not proven. I must give it to you as I see it, now. I believe that Miss Emily Brown was murdered. Someone saw to it that she drank a poison, and she died. I do not believe it was an accident."

A rustle of alarm blew around the room. People braced themselves.

"As a beginning," Duff continued in a quiet voice, "I would like to tell you all why Dr. Norris Christenson thought he had to kill Miss Brown."

No one looked at the doctor. All eyes kept hold of Duff's face, as if they dared not look away. The doctor, himself, shook his head, just a quiver, as if to say unhappily that he still didn't understand.

"The doctor is engaged to Miss Constance Avery"—Duff bowed in that lady's direction—"with whom he is very much in love. Miss Brown had never met Miss Avery. On Sunday evening, last, they were to meet for the first time. During the afternoon, young Taffy, here, took sick, and Miss Brown went across to Mrs. Meredith's house to fetch an ice collar. Waiting there, she stumbled upon a fact she had not known before. She found it out, quite accidentally, I believe,

221

by glancing through an old photograph album, which album I have and can show you. She found out that Dr. Christenson is really Mrs. Meredith's first cousin and the son of Mrs. Meredith's aunt."

Eve covered her face with her hands, suddenly, and fell against the back of her chair. Duff went inexorably on.

"Miss Brown already knew quite well that Mrs. Meredith's aunt had been committed to an asylum, years ago. She died there. I think you can all see, as Miss Brown did, why the doctor went to the trouble of changing his name around a little, and why he hasn't advertised being Eve's cousin. Mrs. Meredith, of course, must have known who he was and kept his secret."

"Of course," groaned Eve. "What did it matter . . . ?"

"Why did he come here, to this town?"

"Because," said Eve, "I helped him. I told my friends he was a good up-and-coming young doctor."

Duff said, "Thank you. Now, Miss Avery, interested as she is in the problems of animal breeding, and therefore in the problems of human heredity, has, from time to time, been quite outspoken in her opinions." Constance's lids trembled.

"The doctor believed, having heard her say so many times, that if she were to be told about his mother's weakness, she would refuse to marry him." Duff let a little pause go by. Miss Avery's breathing was shallow and fast. The doctor sat like a lump. Eve still cowered with a hidden face.

"When Miss Brown, then, showed him the baby picture of himself which she had filched from Eve's album and told him that she had discovered the relationship, do you see his immediate reaction? He desperately wanted to prevent Miss Brown from telling Miss Avery. It was the sort of thing Miss Brown would enjoy doing. She would not, I imagine, respond to any appeal."

The doctor shook his head, involuntarily agreeing.

"Well, he tried, first," Duff went on, "to telephone Miss Avery and cancel the meeting of the two women that was due to take place that evening. But he couldn't reach Miss Avery by phone."

Constance's eyes were lifted, now, with something like hope in them.

"It is too bad that he misunderstood," said Duff blandly. "Too bad that his . . . passion for Miss Avery and his panic lest he lose her conspired to deceive him. He forgot or, at least, did not consider, that a theoretical judgment passed on people in the mass is not always the same judgment that the theorist will make when she considers the individual. Especially," said Duff slyly, "when the individual is herself." Then he was generous. "Miss Avery, of course, would not have thrown him over. She would not have been quite so—shall we say—cold-blooded as that."

A soft sigh escaped Constance. Her eyes fixed on Duff's face were enigmatic. She was not, at least, looking at him as if he were a doorman.

"Well, that was his motive. Miss Brown was quite capable of spilling those beans, would have enjoyed spilling them. And he believed, absolutely, that the spilling of the beans would ruin the rest of his life and take away from him what he most wanted. He was in a panic. Is that clear?"

"O.K." said Pring. "He had a motive, all right. I follow you."

The doctor rubbed his left finger with his right hand, but he did not speak.

"Now, of course, we must try to figure out how he did it. Motive, means, opportunity, the formula goes and must go." Duff settled on his heels. "We have been pretty badly confused about those wine bottles."

"Yeah," muttered Pring.

"By the fingerprints on them, the fact that there were two alike, the evidence of various Moriaritys on the subject. We have been wondering which of them told lies." The Moriarity phalanx bristled perceptibly, all togeher. "However"—Duff smiled at them as if he gave them each a quick reassuring pat of his hand—"let us, for a moment, proceed on the basis that none of the Moriaritys told any lies at all. We have no reason to think that they are liars. We have, instead, the right to assume that they are tellers of the truth, honest and decent and intelligent. And, therefore, able to give evidence that ought to be extremely reliable."

"Yeah, but kids . . ." said Pring.

"Kids," said Duff. "Yes, Davey is a baby; but kids, as you put it, see as clearly as we old fogeys, hear as well. Their eyes and ears are as sharp if not sharper. And their minds are not crusted over with all of our set ideas, either. I, myself, am ready and willing to rely on the sworn evidence of such kids as these. So let us proceed. Suppose we look at the evidence as it has been given and see what it tells us, as is.

"Now, the doctor talked to Brownie, again, in the hall, downstairs. First he had tried to telephone his fiancee. Then Brownie joined him in the hall. She offered him a sip of her wine from the glass she had carried along with her. He did sip it. Dinny saw him do it. He was not harmed. Dinny saw him sip the wine just as she went by on her way upstairs with a tray for her mother. Let us believe that he did so sample it, at that time, and at that time it was merely wine.

"Now, in the next moment, Mary Moriarity called down to Brownie, did she not? To ask about some bacon?"

Dinny nodded. "Yes," said Mary calmly, "I did."

"Miss Brown looked up to where you were and answered?"

"Of course."

"Dinny was upstairs then?"

"Yes."

"I believe it was at that moment, when Miss Brown's attention was directed above her—it was then and there that Dr. Christenson put nicotine sulphate into Brownie's glass."

Eve had uncovered her face to listen better. But no one spoke or moved until the doctor said, as if he were amused, "I see. But how do you figure I had such a thing so handy?"

"I figure you had nicotine sulphate in your pocket because it was nicotine sulphate that killed her," said Duff flatly.

The doctor raised his brows as if to say this was not reasoning.

Duff said, "And I can, of course, imagine how you came to have it in your pocket. What I really believe is that you had bought some nicotine sulphate for Constance Avery, who uses it in connection with her chicken raising. She had none on hand that week end,

225

meant to get some, must have said so. You, doctor, are in the habit of picking up little purchases for her. Aren't you? You bought her some bobby pins, I notice. Where did you buy them? In the dime store?"

The doctor's head nodded yes, as if it did so in spite of himself.

"Then I guess and, in fact, believe, that you picked up the nicotine at the same time, happened to see it on a counter going by. Now, it is not used in medicine. It would not point to a doctor. It is used by gardeners. You knew Mary would have it about the place. It was your choice, rather than any other drug you may have been carrying, for these reasons. It seemed to you an inspiration, eh? It came in very handy."

"Yeah, but you're saying it wasn't in the wine bottle," Robin said, "but listen, Mr. Duff, one of them bottles was poisoned, all right."

"Certainly," said Duff. "Let me go on. Brownie, now holding a glass of poison, walks back to the dining room, tips in a little more wine, drinks it off, and screams in agony. The doctor turns back; Mrs. Moriarity is called down and remains with him until Miss Brown is dead. However—suddenly he insists that Taffy must be rushed to the hospital. Therefore, Mary rushes away upstairs to get her ready. Dinny and the small children have already been sent up there." He turned abruptly and shot out a question. "When did the doctor send you boys outdoors?"

"We were kinda . . . in the hall," said Alfie. "We didn't know what to do. We—"

"I heard him say, 'Mary, I'm afraid she's gone, my dear.' It was right after that. He stuck his head out and said, 'Run outside awhile, you kids.' " One could see

Paul's mind going back, accurately remembering. "Mom was running upstairs as we went."

Duff nodded. "Alfie, did you go to the back porch through the dining room?"

"No, sir. Uh-uh. We weren't supposed to go in there. So I went out the back door and around."

Duff nodded again, as if everything were tumbling nicely into place. "The back door of this house," he said, "is on the side, and going around means quite a little journey. I believe that in that minute or two, the doctor, who was supposed to be speaking on the phone, slipped into the pantry, poured the rest of his poison into the wine bottle, suddenly noticed that another wine bottle stood on the table. Picked up the poisoned one with a handkerchief or a towel or whatever, swiftly changed them. And I think he snapped off the toaster quite automatically, as he did this. Someone did, you know, although he had to deny it."

"*I* lied," said the doctor bitterly.

"Those who commit murder often do," said Duff, unperturbed. "Yes, I believe that the poison was in the bottle before ever Alfie got around the house.

"Now, do you understand those fingerprints? Eve's were on the bottle because it was the bottle that had belonged to her. Brownie's were on it because she brought it into this house and put it in the pantry. Dinny's were on it because she poured some wine from this bottle to take up to her mother. The doctor's were *not* on it, because he saw to it that they didn't get there. He had a reason.

"There were no fingerprints on the other bottle because Mitch wiped them off. There would have been Brownie's and Davey's, at least.

227

"We will believe that Davey did drink some wine. Mitch did wash his glass and wipe off the bottle, as she says. Mitch did not exchange bottles. She could not have erased only her own prints, you know. Nor did she carry it with gloves. She says she didn't, and we believe her. Dinny did pour wine for her mother from the bottle in the pantry. Mary did drink it when it came up on the tray. If we do believe all these things and what the boys have just told us, we find my reconstruction fitting the facts, do we not? Was there any other moment or any other person in which or by whom the thing could have been done? According to evidence?"

The doctor said, "It fits the facts because you've made it up to fit the facts, or what you call the facts, Mr. Duff. You can't prove a single thing you say. Except, of course, that I actually am Eve's cousin. And perhaps that Brownie took the picture. That's all. The rest is fancy guessing. Where is the poison container now? The nicotine sulphate bottle? And why isn't it the one the police have in their possession, the one we *know* was on the premises because it came from Mary's stable?"

"Because that particular little bottle has only Paul's prints on it, and Paul doesn't lie, either. Nor has he falsified evidence." Duff spoke calmly. "I believe you took your little bottle out to your car with you. While you were caught there in the rain, perhaps you washed it out. Perhaps you left it in your car, a clean labelless bottle, and disposed of it later. Oh, you were there in your car, all during the deluge. You hadn't got wet enough. I noticed. You didn't want to be alone downstairs in the Moriarity house, because you knew the wine was poisoned. You wished to seem to have had no chance to get at that bottle of wine."

"You can't prove that. You can't—"

"No," said Duff, "that's true. I can't prove very much. I am telling you what I think."

The doctor said, "I simply do not understand this thing at all. Why do you pick on me? What . . . ?"

"Ah, but I had a dream." Duff leaned on the back of an armchair. He sounded conversational. "I don't mean I dreamed you did it. Not at all. But I have recently made a most interesting psychological discovery. Make a note of it, doctor. When an amateur attempts to interpret a dream, he does not so much analyze the dreamer as he analyzes himself. Try it sometime. Tell three or four people a dream and see what they say. You, doctor, were the only one of four people who thought that the speaker in my dream was a menace *because*, mind you, he could tell or make public or betray something about me. You were the only one who thought that I had locked him up to save myself. And to get a beautiful lady, as a *reward*. It fits your case so well, doesn't it? Someone was going to tell, had to be shut up. Yes.

"Now, your analyses made no contact with any fears of mine. It seemed to me an outlandish interpretation. I tried it on Mr. Haggerty, here. He analyzed the dream again. He put the whole thing in terms of ambition, of making a scoop. Well, he himself is ambitious. I began to catch on. I asked Dinny, who was more objective. A younger and fresher mind, of course. She took it to be a dream of protection, as, indeed, seemed fairly obvious to me."

"Ah," said the doctor. Duff ignored that.

"And Paul," he continued, "was off on another tack. He was very logical and matter of fact, as he *is*. He put it in terms of my business."

The doctor laughed. "Do you think you are going to dream me into jail for a crime I did not do?"

"There is a little more yet," Duff said. "We must remember the poison you put in Eve's icebox, in her coffee-flavored ice cubes which Alfie and Paul so luckily stole before they could damage anyone. And why you did that? You meant to murder Eve, I think."

"You're crazy," said the doctor in disgust. "Coffee-flavored ice . . ." He flapped his hands.

Mary was looking very pale. She hugged her chicks tight.

"Out there on the terrace, yesterday, Miss Avery made quite a clear statement of her views, in front of your cousin Eve, who was offended. It would be almost inhuman for her not to toy with the thought of the revenge she could take on your Constance, would it not? Didn't you fear that she would now be the one to tell Constance about your poor mad mother? Or even wait until you were married and then tell. A nice revenge. And disastrous for you."

Mary leaned forward. "Oh, no!" she said. "No! She *did* think of it. You *were* toying with it, weren't you, Eve? But she never would have told . . . don't you see? Because of Ralph."

"There, again, we nearly had a tragedy," said Duff sadly, "of misunderstanding. You didn't realize that, did you, Doctor? Her son and his welfare are far more important to Mrs. Meredith than a little revenge for an uncomfortable few moments on a summer afternoon. But you were panicky. You'd killed once. You couldn't bear the thought of having done it in vain. So you poisoned the ice."

"But nobody—nothing happened! What do you mean?"

"Oh, no, you didn't succeed, this time. Did you realize," Duff's voice was thin and hard, "that if you had, Mary would have been among your victims? Or didn't you care?" His anger was like iron.

"He suggested that I—come right back," said Mary weakly.

Duff bent his head. "Suggested?" he said quietly. The word fell heavily on their ears.

The doctor said, "You're making all this up, too."

"No," said Duff. "You wouldn't risk letting Constance go. Then I prodded you into a state of hysteria. You told me this yourself. You told me there was danger in the tea party. That's how I knew."

"No."

"Yes."

"No, no, not at all." The doctor stammered eagerly. "I only meant that Constance . . . why, if she wasn't going to mind . . . to mind knowing about my mother . . . she might as well have gone and heard Eve tell about it. Don't you see? Don't you see?"

Pring looked at Duff and rubbed the inside of his cheek with his tongue. Robin smoothed his chin with a big pink hand.

The doctor took heart. "Besides," he cried, "if you think it was Eve they wanted to poison, there's another motive for that. And a better one, I think."

"Indeed?" drawled Duff as if he were bored. He wasn't. He was terrified.

"This is your own fault, Duff," said the doctor.

231

"You know perfectly well that I wouldn't have mentioned any of this, but you'll have to have it now. I've got to fight this—this attack of yours any way I can. With the truth, if necessary."

"Please proceed with the truth," said Duff dryly. No one guessed the fear that closed around and squeezed his heart.

The doctor leaned toward the detectives. They were the jury here. His anxious eyes implored them. "Duff and I both thought and I still think—that little Taffy, the little girl . . ."

Mary put her hands over Taffy's ears and pulled her close. The detectives looked startled. Mr. Haggerty stirred in his corner.

"Now see here," the doctor marked his points with his fingers. "Brownie held the mortgage here, and she wanted money that Mary didn't have. Mary made some remarks at the breakfast table in front of all the kids to the effect that it would be nice if Brownie were dead. Didn't she? You . . . truth-tellers?"

Dinny and the boys nodded their heads and then kept their chins up.

Mary said, "To that effect, perhaps. That's not exactly what I said." She had let go of Taffy's head and was facing this with blazing eyes.

"But Taffy actually said she wished so too?" Mary nodded, a quick sharp nod. "Well," said the doctor, "I think the little girl simply knew no better. Of course she knew about the poison. She had been warned often enough. She knew how to get it. She knew about Brownie and her wine. I think she just did it, because she wished to help her mother and didn't know right from wrong. Also, I'm sure the rest of the family covered up for her. Furthermore, I think Mr. Duff is covering up for her. I know it. Why, he admitted as much to me. A friend of mine, a Mr. O'Leary was in the room. He may remember."

Duff said nothing.

"Now, my point is," continued the doctor, "Eve knows something they can't afford to have told. That's my point. Therefore, I think some one of them"—the Moriarity phalanx seemed to melt into an even firmer unit at his furious gesture—"or . . . who knows? . . . maybe even the famous Mac Duff, in person. . . . I think they wanted Eve to die. Put her out of her misery and save the little one."

"Say, listen," said Pring, "if a kid did it, a kid as young as that . . ."

"Oh, I know, accident, manslaughter—whatever it would be called. But they were frantic!" insisted the doctor.

Duff said softly, swallowing the dread that was like a stone in his gullet, "Would you want your child to go on living with such a brand? Certainly we were frantic."

"Yeah, but murder . . ." Pring looked at him in astonishment.

"They were determined it would never come out!" cried the doctor. "Why, Duff questioned me very closely on what I knew. Fortunately, I didn't admit anything, or *I* might have had a little nicotine in my breakfast food."

"What is this thing you know?" said Duff in what sounded like frank curiosity.

"Why, Taffy had nicotine on her hands," said the doctor. "It can make one ill, you know. I'm sorry. Ask

233

Eve." He fell back. He'd shot his bolt.

Eve was shuddering as if she had been seized by a chill. "It's true!" she moaned. "Oh, Mary, God help you . . . it's true. We found it on her in the hospital. You were talking to the superintendent. I washed it away myself. Norry said not to mention it. I wouldn't have. . . . Mary, forgive me?"

But Mary had no intention of forgiving anybody. She stood up on her two feet. "Oh, don't be ridiculous!" she cried. "*I* washed Taffy's hands. Do you think I don't keep my children clean? Do you think I'd put her to bed . . . ?"

"You can't get it off," gasped Eve, "so easily . . . You mightn't have. . . . It was there!"

But Duff stood beside Mary.

"I do thank you, doctor," he said quietly. "You've convinced me, now, and convicted yourself."

"What . . . ?"

"Didn't I tell you I fell in love with Taffy? I carried her into that hospital room. She was my love, and I kissed her hands. Do you think I would have missed the presence of nicotine? On these little hands?" Duff went down on his knees before Taffy, who looked bewildered almost to tears. He kissed her hands again. "It's all right, sweetheart," he said, and put his head on her warm little knees for a second. "We've got him now."

Mary sat down suddenly. Taffy and Davey began to whimper, feeling emotion present, as little animals might feel it and be affected. Mary hushed them. Duff got up. He looked exhausted.

Pring said, "What's the idea? I don't know if I

follow. . . . He put some stuff on her hands *afterwards*, you mean?"

"That's what I mean," said Duff wearily. "That's what he did. Overdid it. 'Out, out, damned spot!' Play's full of quotations, you know. Oh, if Eve says she saw it, I think we can believe it was there. But *I* didn't see it. So I know it wasn't there when I put her down."

"But *you're* lying! You and Mary!" The doctor was at bay now. "Of course, you'd lie. It's your word against ours. Who's going to decide?"

Mary's face was luminous with faith as she looked at the jury, and Duff stood pat on the truth he knew.

Eve said, "All I know is I saw this brown stain that looked and smelled like tobacco."

"Coal tar from his holder," said Duff carelessly. "Anything, to give the impression. Of course, there's the other nurse."

"What nurse?" said Dr. Christenson.

"The one who was beside me as I put her down." Duff's voice was silk now. "We can inquire."

The doctor was standing. He stood very still. He twisted his head, turning it very slowly, looking around at Eve. He said, slowly, tentatively, "Eve, did you put something on her hands? Did you . . . ?"

Eve froze. She sat in her crouching rigidity.

Pring cleared his throat.

Miss Constance Avery got up suddenly. She said, sounding as tired as Duff had sounded, "There's no use, is there, Mr. Duff? He did it. We were together in his car this morning, and he left me in the back lane to go into Eve's house. When he came out he said she had already gone to the funeral. But he was in there. This morning. Do you understand?"

"Another link," said Duff. "Thank you."

But the doctor was looking at Constance, first in incredulous horror, then in rage. "Keep your mouth shut, you damned bitch!" he screamed and dove across at her. "You'd betray me, would you? Would you? I did it for you!" he sobbed. "You're to blame . . . You're the one . . ."

Alfie got him by the left leg and held on like a plump bulldog. Paul twisted one of his arms back, expertly. Paul was very strong. Yet it took Duff and Robin, too, to pull him finally away and let Constance fall, mussed and terrified, into Mary's pitying arms.

The doctor was crying tears and beating his hands on the floor.

"O.K., Mr. Haggerty," said Duff, panting. "Here's your reward . . . your dream comes true. I guess you scooped the story."

"Holy smokes!" said Mr. Haggerty, biting a half-inch clean off his pencil. "That's right! I got it! Where's the telephone?"

"Mommy," said Taffy a little later, "was he bad? Are they going to put him in jail?"

"Yes, darling. At least they'll put him somewhere where he can't hurt anybody any more. He was very bad."

Taffy sobbed once. She was a little upset, but she was adjusting. Duff squeezed her fingers.

"He was awfully bad," said Davey. He wiggled off the couch and stood in front of them with his ears like cup handles and his funny little face with its soft baby nose screwed up fiercely. "He put bad poison in Brownie's glass."

236

Duff started to speak, but Mary put out her hand. "How do you know, babe?" she said to Davey.

"I saw him," said Davey. "Whin they were out in the hall."

"Davey, you didn't!"

"I did so!"

"He must have heard what you said . . ."

"But I could see," said Davey. "He put the glass down on top of the radiator."

Duff had a sudden vision of that handy, flat-topped radiator and the doctor using two hands on the little bottle. But Paul struck himself on the forehead, and Dinny rolled her eyes. Alfie made queer noises through his teeth. Mitch said, aghast, "I'll betcha he did!"

Davey said, airily, "I certainly certainly did."

The Moriaritys and Duff looked at each other in wonder and despair.

"We'll never *know*," said Dinny.

"He's a peanut," said Paul sighing.

CHAPTER 18

Everyone had gone away.

Mr. Haggerty had babbled a long time into the phone and gone away in a happy hurry.

Eve had been calm. It was as if she spent her life in training for crises, and now that one had come, she was ready. She was prepared. She had watched them take the doctor out, seeming to be quietly resigned. It was Constance, unprepared, who fell to pieces. A disheveled, unstrung Constance who wept and began to blurt out hopes and fears and disappointments in one great breakdown of reserve. Duff had encouraged her to go home. He had encouraged Eve to take her there.

It was, he felt as they went, the beginning of a beautiful friendship. One lonely female would find another who was willing to hear all about it and probably agree that men, on the whole, were louses. Eve, full of pity and strength, seemed not to be worrying, yet, about Ralph. Perhaps she would, later.

Duff felt she would, unless her time could be taken up otherwise. She was one to fill the vacuums in her life with worry. He hoped these two could ally themselves against an empty world. He was sorry, in his happiness, for all troubled souls.

But when he telephoned Mr. O'Leary, he broke the news quickly and coldly and left that gentleman high and dry with his disillusionment. Duff wanted no part of any transference, of any devotion from that quarter. He was quite selfish about it. All he wanted, at the moment, was to clear everything and everyone away and have a quiet supper with the Moriaritys.

They scratched a supper together, ate it in the bare-floored dining room. Afterward, Taffy and Davey got put to bed with ceremony. Duff was included. Everybody except Duff seemed to take this very much for granted. After Davey had been pommeled by Paul, had his toes tweaked by Alfie, had been smacked on either cheek by his big sisters, it was Duff who must lean over and feel the baby nose pushed into his cheek while the airy kiss landed in the air.

"Good night, Davey."

"Good night, Mr. Mac Duff."

Mary patted her smallest, seeming to mold him into a sleepy knot. Then they all trooped into Taffy's room.

Paul said, all gentleness, "Good night, sweetheart." Duff had to choke down the rush of feeling in his throat. After all the tension and relief he could have blubbered to see Taffy receiving, like blessings, the love that belonged to her and doing it like a little queen, not arrogant, but sweet and sure. He added his own, humbly. He loved them all, but Taffy was the rose of the world.

He was still a bit exalted when he and Mary and the four bigger ones gathered in the shabby living room where Brownie had died and where her murderer had lost control and given himself up and been taken away. Now, with windows open to the evening air, it was cool and homely.

"How did you know?" they besieged him.

"That's going to be hard to say," Duff confessed. He was eased into a big chair. He looked at home there. He felt at home, and his heart was tender toward them. "There were a couple of things that kept bothering me," he told them. He didn't much want to think of clues, and his mind groped reluctantly back. "For instance," he said, "I kept wondering why he hustled Taffy off to the hospital. It didn't seem as necessary as all that. He jumped at a chance to get Mary out of the way, to muddle things with crisis and comings and goings."

"So he could get at the wine bottle?"

"Partly that. He went through the kitchen, I think, following inside the house the course the boys were taking outside. He fixed the wine in the pantry, nipped in and changed bottles. Thereafter, he was on the phone, and as quickly as possible out of the house. He was going to take Taffy himself. He'd be gone."

"Leaving the children," said Mary suddenly.

Duff said, "His concern for the children didn't exist except in reverse. Of course, he tried to make it seem that he feared for Taffy, wanted to get her away before the police came, because she might betray herself. For that," he added quietly, "I do not forgive him."

"Nor I," said Mary, just as quietly. "Is he insane, do you think?"

"No," said Duff. "I don't think so. But he may be. I wouldn't be the one to say. All along, you know, he thought of Taffy as his way out. He thought she could take his guilt, if necessary, without suffering. I suppose it was his idea of doing no harm." Mary looked simply grim and said nothing, nor did the kids. "For that we do not forgive him," repeated Duff, "but let's see . . . what else. Of course, there was my famous dream. His analysis was so fantastically unrelated to anything in my mind, I was forced to wonder from whose mind it came. He was very careless. Of course, O'Leary adored him and hung on his words. O'Leary had made the doctor his personal savior. Nervous cases do that, often. Usually the savior is the psychiatrist who treats them. O'Leary was a devoted barnacle who both flattered and puzzled Christenson, but who was his great audience before whom he couldn't resist performing. Yes, he was careless.

"Naturally, I didn't see all this in any flash. But it bothered me. I told the dream to Haggerty, half in fun. After what he said, the thing bothered me still more."

"Then we analyzed it," said Dinny.

"Who was right?" asked Paul as if there were a certain answer.

"Oh, I think you were. That is, you and Dinny." Duff went on quickly. "Then again, I couldn't help wondering why on earth Brownie would be packing that baby picture around the country with her. It ought to be significant. But I couldn't guess how. Oh, I had some pretty fantastic thoughts, plenty of them. I thought maybe he had lied, and it wasn't his picture at all."

"Oh, I knew it was," said Mary. "At least, I knew it

241

was supposed to be, and that Brownie had had it for a long time."

"I ought to have asked you," murmured Duff. "Then, I thought Brownie was in love with him, perhaps."

"No," said Mary, "not exactly. You . . . hit it right."

"She liked him," said Dinny.

"Sure she did," said Paul.

"But she didn't really like anybody very much," said Mitch suddenly and wisely. She had put herself close to Duff's knee. He had a shaky feeling that even this wild spirit was letting him draw close. He smiled down and said, "No." All the eyes looked thoughtful.

"Say, listen, was his car really on the blink in all that rain?" demanded Alfie. "Or was he lying about that?"

"I believe it was genuinely on the blink," said Duff. "I think he really wanted to get out of the house himself, a kind of alibi after the fact, you see? I do believe it was the hand of—the rain that drew me into this."

"Lucky for us," said Dinny warmly.

"And how!" echoed the boys.

Duff said, "Good luck is better than good management. For God knows I wasn't managing this case. I was all mixed up."

"Ha ha," said Alfie, without mirth but politely.

"No, I meant that," said Duff. "I stumbled into nearly every telling stroke. I didn't like Constance Avery. I simply did not like the woman. I had a mean desire to give her her come-uppance. So, when I wanted to shake the doctor up, I chose to do it by attacking her. Because she annoyed me. Malice. Or else some good subconscious angel. For only by

242

attacking Constance could I have got that hint about the tea party at Eve's."

"Hint? What hint?"

"Why, the doctor said—it slipped out hysterically—'Maybe, I should have let her go to the tea party.' "

"But he explained that," objected Dinny.

"He tried to explain it. But if the thought in his mind had been what he later claimed it was—mark his words. Look at his language. Remember his state. Wouldn't he have said, 'Why, I *could* have let her go to the tea party,' or 'I *might as well* have let her go.' Not, 'Maybe I *should* have. . . .' No, that meant what I heard it mean. Danger."

Dinny nodded. Her lips moved over the phrases, an actress testing lines.

"So you ran," said Paul, grinning.

"You sure did run!"

"Gosh!"

"You flew!"

"I wish you coulda seen yourself go over the gate!"

"With all my leaping and bounding, I was too late," said Duff sadly.

"But it turned out all right." The kids sighed happily.

"More luck," he said.

Mary disagreed, boldly. "I shouldn't call it luck when you stood here and maintained we wouldn't lie, the way you did."

"Oh, that was wonderful!" cried Dinny. "It felt good. Didn't it?"

"Yeah," the boys admitted. And Mitch wriggled.

Dinny said, "And we don't, as a general rule. Even

243

Davey just makes things up. He doesn't really lie."

"Oh, making things up doesn't count," said Duff, smiling at her. "Hessians, for instance." Everybody looked at Dinny for a moment. Then Duff went on. "All I could do was state my own faith," he murmured. "After all, my faith has a right to get stated. It's got as good a chance as anybody's to be justified."

"Better," said Paul, with admiration.

"Though scarcely scientific," Duff murmured.

"Science," said Mary suddenly, looking straight at him, "isn't all it takes." His heart left out a beat and went on faster.

But Alfie was squirming now. "Yeah, but even so, I don't see why it couldn't be Aunt Eve. I mean, gosh, it could have been. She's so kinda unbuttoned most of the time, you wouldn't put it past her."

"Being unbuttoned, though distressing, is no crime," said Duff. "But don't you see that if I believed your mother, who said she drank the wine, then the wine with Eve's fingerprints came innocent into this house? And since Eve hadn't been here to make any new fingerprints, it wasn't Eve."

"Oh," said Dinny. "Well, of course mother wouldn't lie."

"No," said Duff, "I know."

Mary said, a little hastily, "Look here, you kids, what I want to know is what you've been up to. All these monkey shines with ice cubes. What on earth . . . ?"

"Well, gosh," said Alfie, "we heard them say it must be an inside job, nobody else in the house. We couldn't let them get away with that!"

"We thought we'd better mix things up a little," said Paul.

"And we did, too," said Dinny, "for a while." She looked at Duff out of the corner of her eye. "Of course, we didn't know Mr. Duff so well, then."

Duff laughed. "You and your Hessian! Making out you were covering up with a fake ghost, while all the while you wanted me to think that was what you were doing!"

"And you did!"

"Oh, yes, I thought," confessed Duff, "what you wanted me to think. You were acting. It took me a while to find out that you were acting as *if* you were acting, too." His heart began to beat fast again. "Of course," he said casually, "I thought you were concealing your father here."

"Dad!"

"Who else?" Duff asked.

"Ye gods!" said Dinny. "We never even thought of that."

"But Dad doesn't come near us any more. He's married—"

"Yes, I know, now. At least I . . ."

"But what made you think . . . ?"

"How?"

"Why?"

Duff didn't look at Mary. He told the kids. "I got a bit haunted by my Professor Moriarity. Do you know, I thought perhaps our friend, Mr. Haggerty, was he?"

They giggled.

"Or again, I thought a Mr. Severson, who was hiding from the law, was really your father and was hiding here." They gaped. "After all, if he was hiding, I had to imagine why, didn't I?"

Mitch pitched backward and sprawled on the floor. It was like the last frame in a comic strip. She left the "Pow!" behind her. "Oh, my goodness!" beamed Dinny, rocking.

"I'm breaking down all your illusions," said Duff ruefully. "I'm showing myself up. Why, I even went so far off the track as to think for one moment, there in the garden, that Mr. O'Leary was your father. I soon came to and remembered that he couldn't be."

"Couldn't be?"

"It was impossible."

"Why?"

"Because Mr. O'Leary has blue eyes."

"Hm?"

"Mitch's are brown. So are yours, Dinny. So are Alfie's."

"Mendelian Law," said Paul. "Why, sure. Look at Mom."

Mary's puzzled eyes were bluer than ever.

"Oh," said the twins together.

Mitch sat up. "What's the Mendelian Law?"

"Never mind. Wait till you get to high school," said Dinny. "Go on."

But Duff didn't go on. He said evasively, "However, Mr. Haggerty and Mr. Severson both had brown eyes, and so have many other people."

They sighed. Mary hadn't said much.

Alfie wriggled with delight, and his feet massaged each other. "Yeah, but we fooled you that first night, huh? With the bathroom."

Mary woke up. "The what?"

Dinny surrounded words with laughter. "Oh, Lord, Mother, you know what Paul did? He put a fishline around the handle of the t-toilet up in the front bathroom and hung it down out the window and went and pulled it, so the toilet flushed, but we were all right there, where he could *see* it wasn't us. . . ."

"Paul was standing in the front door," said Alfie. "We tried to keep Mr. Duff looking at Davey."

"I nearly died," said Dinny. "Davey was wonderful!"

"Y'see, the fishline was double," said Paul. "After it worked I just whipped the line away by pulling only one end. That was while he was chasing upstairs."

"Aren't we devils!" squealed Dinny.

"You are," said Duff placidly. "And the fishline hung down to be within reach. So Mr. Haggerty bumped into it. He brushed his face. I did think of that later, you know. And I wondered why . . . er . . . after all there is a bathroom on the third floor for the use of ghosts. I suppose you used the same fishline method on the rocking chair?"

"Sure," said Paul. "First we lured you to go up there. Then I ran around and yanked it. The window only had to be up a tiny crack. I had a little block in there. You *couldn't* notice," he soothed.

Duff said, "I didn't . . . er . . . notice at the time."

Mary cried, "You monkeys!" Her eyes were boldly laughing into Duff's, and his responded.

"Of course, we had to tell Davey to have an earache," said Dinny. "Did you know that? I mean, that first night?"

"Sure," said Alfie, "he had to be downstairs, too, or you'd have thought it was Davey. Going to the bathroom."

"I'd have thought it was Davey," said Duff slowly. "Yes, I heard you say so, although I didn't know, at the time, what you meant. Tell me, was it you, Mitch, who went down the clothes chute about midnight?"

"Sure," Mitch tossed her head.

"It was her own idea," said Alfie proudly. "She can do it. Only she can't stop at the second floor. She has to go all the way down to the cellar."

Duff had a vision of this tiny girl sliding through the walls in the dark, arms above her head, toes pointed, and, doubtless, the ballerina's faint smile on her lips.

Mitch said, "It's fun. It's easy." She looked as if she might get up now and go do it again.

"One of these days," said Mary, not very solemnly, "you'll gain a pound and get stuck."

"We'll have to tear the wall out," said Paul calmly. Mitch smiled as if she knew what she knew.

"I suppose you sneaked up to bed while I was on the third floor?" asked Duff. "Yes, I guessed that, finally. You took a key?"

"I got locked in the cellar once by sliding down that way," said Mitch airily. "I thought I'd better take a key. 'Course, any old key will fit that cellar door."

Mary's mouth was part open.

"She did it to make mysterious footsteps," Duff explained to her. "Does Mitch like movies?"

"Why?"

"Oh . . . for a minute, there was a certain rhythm. . . ." Duff hummed a little tune.

Mitch looked him in the eye for a moment, dead

pan, and then her face broke and she giggled. "I thought somebody had a sense of humor," said Duff. "Anybody want to confess to smoking a cigarette on the second floor while I was running around downstairs being baffled?"

"You did notice!" cried Dinny in triumph. "I *thought* you would. They said, go on, you wouldn't notice. *I* did that!"

"Dinny!" said Mary in somewhat absent-minded reproof.

"Well, I've smoked, Mother. So has Paul, but he doesn't like to."

"The boys attended to the eggshells, I presume?" Duff said.

"Eggshells!"

"Eggshells outside my window in the morning."

"That was me," said Paul modestly.

"But I ate em!" claimed Alfie.

"Well, I boiled them," said Dinny.

"Oh, dear! You must have had a dreadful time!" said Mary. "Such goings-on!"

"I did have a dreadful time," said Duff without reproach. "Still, my obsession with . . . er . . . Professor Moriarity drove me to hunt for his picture. And so I found Eve's album. Good out of evil cometh, or the moral is luck, again."

"But did you ever find Dad's picture?"

"Oh, yes."

"And it wasn't Mr. Haggerty, so you felt better?"

"I felt a lot better," said Duff. "You see, it turned out to be the picture of a Mr. Walker, whom I'd met."

"Walker?"

"Oh, goodness, is he Walker now?"

"Yes. He was at the hospital when I came out. And, Lord, how I should have known!"

"Why? Why should you?" they pressed.

"Because he told me all your real names."

"He did?"

"All of them. Reeled them off with your right ages. Paul, Diana, Alfred, Margaret, Rosamund, David. Like that."

"*He* oughta know," said Paul.

"I guess he ought," said Dinny. "I guess practically nobody else would be so sure. We're quite a family for nicknames. I mean, me and Mitch and Taffy, anyhow."

"You're quite a family," said Duff affectionately. "Also, of course, his—the woman he was with—said something that hinted at the theater. She said, 'What is this small-town routine?' Routine. That's a kind of act, isn't it?"

"I'll bet he *was* acting," said Dinny, nodding.

"Um," Duff murmured. "Besides, he told me he worked nights. But, Lord, I saw signs of the theater in everyone. Haggerty's act, a role he creates for himself out of sheer romance . . ."

"Denis is married again," said Mary. "I thought you knew."

"No," said Duff. "Of course, after I recognized him, I knew he had been busy having a minor accident. And his interest in all of you was kind but . . . vague. Somehow, I didn't suspect him any more. Meanwhile, of course, I had gone past the picture in the album that was really significant. The one with the round flower bed. I went back to see if it was the same. It was." Duff opened his hands. "I don't think there's any more to tell you."

"You found out Mr. Haggerty's really a reporter, huh?"

"Mr. Haggerty is ambitious. He's pretty fiercely romantic about it. I expect he is trying to be suave. Mr. O'Leary, of course, is a nervous man who fastened his faith on Dr. Christenson. Too absorbed in himself, he was, to stop reading up on symptoms and listen to our troubles. Until we touched on mental troubles, of course." The kids all looked very wise, and Duff smiled to himself. "And Mr. Severson is a Mr. Patrini. He's been caught again and will, we hope, have justice done him. The ghost is gone. All clear?"

"I guess so," sighed Alfie in regret. "Gee . . ."

"Who wants a Coke?" said Paul.

"Mother, can we have some of those chocolate cookies?"

"The sky's the limit," said Mary. The kids clattered off to the kitchen.

"Luck," thought Duff. He leaned across, as if he couldn't help it, and touched Mary's hand. She twisted her fingers up for a moment in a miniature handclasp and drew them away.

"Denis . . ." she began.

"I haven't asked . . ."

"But let me tell you," she insisted, and then she brooded a moment. "You asked me whether he was a handsome rascal. Well, he was. He was fun. He was full of whims and impulses and charm. He used to like us to drop everything and run off to do something gay or silly. In the middle of the night or in the middle of the morning or any old time. He'd take a notion to drop everything that was sober or dutiful—he'd say the hell with it.

"In those days there was such a thing as servants. So I'd often go. This was my mother's house before it was mine. I had old-time reliable servants. I used to go.

"But he was always running away, dropping things, saying the hell with it. Wanting to wipe out the past and start over again, somehow. He thought that was adventurous. Living dangerously or something. I don't know."

She was silent a moment. "But it got so darned monotonous!" she wailed.

"What?" Duff sat up.

"I must be queer," said Mary almost angrily, "but working at things, and keeping the same line, and building up and hanging on, that just seems to me more *interesting* than being so goldarned carefree. I never minded a little care! I *like* it!"

Duff laughed out loud.

She seemed satisfied that he'd understood, so far. "I know," she went on seriously, "you thought it was strange I had no pictures."

"No, I . . ." Duff stammered. "Perhaps it was because you didn't want to be reminded. . . . I . . . Eve did the same."

"Not at all," said Mary crisply. "You see, Denis hated snapshots. He avoided them. All his pictures were taken professionally for professional purposes. So . . . well, he took them with him when he left. You see, some of them were young. He couldn't bear to give them up. I didn't care."

Duff bowed his head.

"But I loved him for quite a while," she said quietly, "as long as I . . . as we could. And the kids are so fine. They've got some of his best in them. I still think kindly of him. He lives the way he wants to live. He saw I couldn't, any more. I live the way I like. Do you see? I suppose we still . . . love each other as much as we can. But it's better from afar."

Her eyes were clear and calm and confiding. Duff said, "Thank you, Mary." He looked very peaceful. "And, of course, you had your children," he murmured, "to love and to raise and to keep you interested. And you put out of your head any idea of marrying again."

"But I had to," she cried. "Who'd want to marry a grass widow with six children!"

He smiled.

"Oh," she cried, "I didn't mean . . . I didn't want . . . No."

"Mary, darling, I do love your children. They're charming in themselves, and they're part of your charm, too. But I love you most. There was a beautiful lady in my dream, Mary. Paul said maybe it was some dame I was in love with . . . 'or your mother or something.' That was when I knew it was *his* mother, the most beautiful dame he could think of, or I, either. Marry me. Or at least let me hang around while you examine the idea, now that I've put it in your head."

Mary said, "Oh, please . . . I didn't . . ." Then her blue gaze came up, and she melted his heart with her lovely sincerity. "Mr. Duff . . ." she said. "I mean, Mac . . . MacDougal . . . You must know you have made it absolutely impossible for me ever to tell you even the shadow of a lie. I . . . I like you very well. I know you

253

love the children. I *will* examine the idea. I can't help it. It . . . startles me, now. But I think . . . if you do mean it . . . after a while . . . I'll . . . we'll . . . you'll . . .

"Oh!" she cried, "you *know* what's going to happen!"

Duff didn't say whether he had known. But he knew now, and he gathered her in.

Meanwhile, the kids came back from the kitchen and stood in the archway with their Coke bottles, watching with solemn eyes.

"My goodness," said Dinny, very innocent and unperturbed, "did the ghost show up again? Or what?"

"You go to bed," said Mary, "the lot of yez!"

DON'T MISS THESE OTHER
BERKLEY MEDALLION LARGE-TYPE
MYSTERIES

ARTISTS IN CRIME   (N2105—95¢)
  by Ngaio Marsh

TO LOVE AND BE WISE   (N2054—95¢)
  by Josephine Tey

DO NOT FOLD, SPINDLE OR   (S2177—75¢)
  MUTILATE
  by Doris Miles Disney

WHEN IN ROME   (N2157—95¢)
  by Ngaio Marsh

METHOD IN MADNESS   (S2184—75¢)
  by Doris Miles Disney

AND, COMING SOON:

TRICK OR TREAT   (S2207—75¢)
  by Doris Miles Disney

STRAW MAN   (N2233—95¢)
  by Doris Miles Disney

(Please turn page)

OR THESE LARGE-TYPE GOTHIC NOVELS

KINGDOM'S CASTLE   (S2153-75¢)
  by Daoma Winston

THE BRIDE OF GAYLORD   (S2084—75¢)
  HALL
  by Saliee O'Brien

HANDS OF TERROR   (S2174—75¢)
  by Jeanne Crecy

DOOR INTO TERROR   (S2183—75¢)
  by Juanita Coulson

THE RELUCTANT WIDOW   (Z2159—$1.25)
  by Georgette Heyer

SYLVESTER   (Z2163—$1.25)
  by Georgette Heyer

AND, COMING SOON:

THE KEY TO HAWTHORN   (S2205—75¢)
  HEATH
  by Afton Patricia Huff

Send for a *free* list of all our books in print

These books are available at your local newsstand, or send
price indicated plus 15¢ per copy to cover mailing costs
to Berkley Publishing Corporation, 200 Madison Avenue,
New York, N. Y. 10016.